CONNELL

A CAROLINA REAPERS NOVEL

SAMANTHA WHISKEY

By Samantha Whiskey

ALSO BY SAMANTHA WHISKEY

The Seattle Sharks Series:

Grinder

Enforcer

Winger

Rookie

Blocker

Skater

Bruiser

Wheeler

Defender

The Carolina Reapers Series:

Axel

Sawyer

Connell

A Modern-Day Fairytale Romance:

The Crown

The Throne

NOW AVAILABLE IN AUDIOBOOK!

Grinder
Enforcer
Winger
Rookie

Let the Seattle Sharks spice up your morning commute!

To those who need to laugh, and to the ones who go out of their way to ensure we do

CONNELL

*S*tifling, oppressive heat smacked me in the face as I stepped out of the Jag in front of the Sweet Water courthouse. Not that the tiny building just off Main Street was much to boast about, but whatever happened here today determined if I got to go home to Scotland next week. Charleston, and the little town of Sweet Water—where myself and the rest of my NHL team made our homes—was lovely most of the year, but I'd rather be in the highlands than sweating my balls off during the off-season.

"Just let me do the talking," Gregory Chastain, my over-priced, pretentious prick of a lawyer instructed as he fell into step next to me.

"Considering that's what I pay ye for, I figured I'd sit back and watch it play out," I told him as we walked through the door. Thank you, sweet mother of Christ, the air conditioning was in perfect working order.

"Right, and that's what you said last time in Miami, remember?" He cocked an eyebrow and straightened his tie.

"The other lawyer was being a daft—"

"Connell!" Langley, the head of public relations for the

Carolina Reapers, came down the small hallway, her heels clicking on the stone floor. Her black hair was tied up in a professional-looking twist, which told me this wasn't a social call. "Glad you boys made it on time."

"I was just telling Connell to keep his commentary to a minimum," Gregory drawled.

"On that point, we agree." Langley's lips flattened.

"What's got ye frazzled?" I asked. If Langley was worried, there had to be a reason. The woman was cool and calm even when shit hit the fan. Considering she was married to my Captain, Axel Nyström, she knew how to handle her fair share of Reaper drama.

"Oh, nothing, as long as we can get in there a few minutes early. The judge is ready, so if you guys are, we can move this right along." She nodded and motioned toward the double doors that separated the sparse waiting area from the courtroom.

"I'm fine with that," Gregory agreed.

"Let's get this over with." I adjusted the wrists of my sleeves under my jacket. Going to court meant breaking out the big guns, also known as my gray Armani suit.

We entered the court—wait, was this really a courtroom? There were folding chairs set up in rows, then two tables each with two chairs, and a larger table on what looked to be a small stage.

"It doubles as the community center," Langley explained in hushed tones as an older woman carrying a laptop entered the room from the door toward the back—on the side of the stage. "They only hear cases in here once a week."

"Between bingo and dodgeball?" I asked.

She rolled her eyes. "Don't. Not today. No jokes. No humor. No excuses. Yes, sir. No, sir. You get the point."

This time my eyes were the ones rolling. "Aye, Langley. I understand."

Gregory and I took our seats at the right-hand table, and Langley took one of the folding chairs behind us as an officer walked in the same door the woman had used.

They talked for a moment as she set up her laptop, and I tried not to twiddle my thumbs. Had I been an idiot? Sure, but this wasn't anything a ten-thousand-dollar check and an apology couldn't fix.

"Carson, it's good to see you," the woman said with a soft smile as a middle-aged man in a suit took the table opposite ours.

"The city attorney," Gregory whispered. "He's really just after restitution. Don't worry."

"All rise, the honorable Judge Neil Hurston presiding," the officer said in a deep, drawling voice.

We stood, and the chairs made a God-awful shriek against the gym floor.

The judge walked out onto the stage like he was here for a Saturday matinee. His glasses slipped down his nose, but he pushed them back up as he took his seat at the table.

He banged his gavel. Why? Like there were dozens of people here to bring to order? "And we're in session. Why don't y'all sit down?"

We sat. Some people thought my Scottish accent was thick—probably because it was, but I had nothing on a few of these Southerners around here, this judge included.

"Carson, what do you have for me today?" Judge Hurston asked.

The other lawyer walked up to the stage and handed the officer—apparently the bailiff—a packet of papers, which he forwarded to the Judge.

"Your honor, we're here in the matter of the Town of Sweet Water versus Connell MacDhuibh—"

"MacDhuibh," I corrected his pronunciation. There was no need to butcher my name while we were at it.

3

Every gaze swung my way.

"MacDhuibh," I said again, slowly. "You doona really say the 'h.'"

Gregory's sigh could have blown away the tablecloth if we'd had one.

"Right," Carson said slowly. "MacDhuibh."

"That's better," I said with a nod.

The judge looked over his glasses at me, but there was a slight smile as he shook his head. "Go ahead, Carson."

"Right, as I was saying. On the night of June ninth, Mr. MacDhuibh," he paused and looked my way until I nodded. Guy's pronunciation was shite, but it would do. "Did drive his four-wheeler at irresponsible speeds down Main Street, at which point he lost control of his vehicle—"

"I swerved to avoid a wee rabbit," I said to Gregory.

He shot me a glare. Guy probably would have elbowed me into silence had we not been in the middle of a court-room...community center...thing.

"—causing a crash that resulted in a great deal of damage to—"

The door opened behind us and shut with a god-awful slam.

"You started without me?" The sweetest southern accent I'd ever heard in my life filled the community center, bouncing off the empty walls. Unfortunately, that sweet little voice belonged to the biggest pain in my arse I'd ever known.

Annabelle Clarke.

"Ms. Clarke, we were all in attendance and decided to start early," Carson explained with a slight cringe.

"Well, I *never*." She came into my peripheral vision and stopped just behind Carson's table—the same row as Langley but definitely not the same side.

"Annabelle, as the city clerk, you are not required to be at

4

every case this court hears." Judge Hurston leaned back in his seat like he needed to settle in for the long-haul.

"Well, I certainly want to be present at *this* one!" She fisted her hands on her hips, and I gave into temptation, leaning back past Gregory to look at her.

The lass was bonnie, and that wasn't a term I used lightly —certainly not since moving to America when I got drafted.

Her brown hair curled in thick waves that made my hands twitch as if they knew how soft it would feel. God, the woman was built for sin. That prim, tailored suit only accented the curves that starred in most of my x-rated fantasies lately. She wasn't stick-thin like so many of the puck-bunnies that wiggled themselves into my lap at every opportunity. No, Annabelle was shaped like she'd been put on this earth purely to drive me bat-shit crazy—all soft skin, ample curves, thick, grippable hips, and breasts that belonged on a porn star.

Not that proper, orderly, stick-up-her-ass Annabelle Clarke ever watched porn with those big brown eyes—no, those were for spotting every single violation of the home owner's association covenants or city ordinances possible. God, were they beautiful eyes, with thick, dark lashes.

Eyes that were currently glaring daggers into me over a lush mouth painted the most irresistible color of red. I bet she'd leave amazing prints on my—

"He destroyed our beloved Oliver!"

I did *what*?

"What are you blethering about, woman?" I asked, earning me a blistering look from Gregory.

Annabelle scoffed. "Oliver! Our cherished statue!"

"You named the bloody ostrich statue?" The woman might be the most fuckable piece of womanhood I'd ever seen, but damn was she daft.

5

"Take this seriously!" Langley hissed as she leaned forward and swatted my shoulder.

"I didn't name it! The town did in 1933!" Annabelle exclaimed.

"Annabelle, sit down," Judge Hurston ordered.

She shot me another quick glare but did as he bid.

"Carson, you were saying?" Judge Hurston finished with a sigh.

Carson shot Annabelle a look that said he clearly wasn't comfortable with her sitting behind him, and then cleared his throat. "Right. Mr. MacDhuibh's drag race—"

"Which I was winning," I muttered under my breath, earning me another swat from Langley.

"—ended when he crashed into the ostrich statue."

"Oliver!" Annabelle corrected.

Carson's shoulders dipped. "Oliver," he repeated with exasperation.

"Son, were you hurt?" Judge Hurston asked me.

"Bruised shoulder and broken ego, sir, but that's all." I bit back the instinct to tell him I wasn't his son. Or any man's son in any way but the most biological sense of the word.

"Glad to hear it. Carson, what are the damages to the statue?" The judge flipped through the papers he'd been handed earlier.

"It's about nine thousand in damages, but we're waiting on one last estimate from a local company to be sure. It's only the pedestal that's affected—"

"A *priceless* pedestal!" Annabelle seethed.

Judge Hurston looked over his glasses at her, and she folded her arms under her breasts. If that neckline was just an inch lower, I would have had a whole new fantasy to work with tonight.

"Your Honor, if I may?" Gregory interjected.

"Please do," the judge answered.

"My client is prepared to pay any and all damages to the statue. He acknowledges his—"

"Idiocy?" Annabelle suggested sweetly.

"—mistake. I'm sure you know that June ninth was the day of the Stanley Cup parade, and my client is the first to admit that he was so overcome by that experience that his judgment was impaired."

"Impaired by alcohol is more like it," Annabelle quipped.

"He wasn't drinking, Annabelle," Carson retorted. "We have his toxicology report. For the love of God, would you like my job?"

Her cheeks ripened to a shade of pink just darker than the suit she wore. Her eyes flickered toward mine, and she mouthed, "sorry," to Langley. Not me.

Hard to believe those two were friends, but since Annabelle happened to be the best friend of Echo Hayes—the fiancée of our goalie, Sawyer, they weren't exactly strangers. The women who put up with us Reapers weren't only gorgeous and smarter than we were—they were thick as bloody thieves.

"As I was saying," Gregory brought us back on track. "Mr. MacDhuibh recognizes his fault and is willing to do whatever the court deems necessary to make it right."

"I will take that into account, Mr. Chastain. Carson, is the city satisfied with reparations in this matter?"

"We are, your honor."

"We are *not!*" Annabelle blurted, coming to her feet. Surprisingly dainty feet at that.

"Annabelle!" Carson groaned.

"Judge, if I may?" she asked sweetly, stepping into the aisle.

"Well, it's not like any of us can stop you, apparently," Judge Hurston drawled with a long-winded sigh. "Come on up."

She walked right past us, and I kept my eyes off her arse. Barely.

"Your Honor, this man has no understanding of our community—"

"Objection!" Gregory exclaimed, standing quickly.

"Mr. Chastain, we're not that formal around here, but go ahead," Judge Hurston waved him on.

"My client is a homeowner here in Sweet Water. He's invested in the community—"

"Hardly! He lives in Reaper Village, sure, but invested? Don't you think that's a bit of a stretch?" She turned a glare on Gregory that would have made a weaker man's balls wither.

"I have over nine million dollars invested in Sweet Water Bank and Trust. I'd call that an investment," I retorted. That wasn't counting what I had put away in stocks and ventures.

Her jaw dropped, but she quickly recovered. "Money isn't what I'm talking about, Mr. MacDhuibh."

I grinned at her spot-on pronunciation. Lass had to have practiced, which meant she'd thought about me when I wasn't around. Maybe it wasn't in a favorable light, but I could work with that. "Well, what are you talking about?"

She blinked rapidly and turned an even darker shade of pink.

"While we here in Sweet Water are incredibly proud to be the home of the Reapers, we'd like you to be proud to be a resident of Sweet Water. That's not about money, Mr. MacDhuibh."

Connell. Och, I wanted to hear my name on those lips.

"I'm already a proud resident of Sweet Water."

"How can that be when you don't know a stitch of our history? You didn't even know that ostrich racing saved this town during the great depression."

8

Surely, I heard that wrong. "You used to race those great big birds?"

"I didn't, of course. It's actually rather inhumane, but in the thirties, those ostrich races brought in the only income our little town could count on." Her fists landed on her hips again. "You can't make this up to us by replacing what you broke. We don't want or need your money."

"Actually—" Carson started.

"Shh," Annabelle threw her finger out at him without breaking eye contact with me. "What we want—no, what we *demand* is your respect."

"I respect you just fine," I assured her.

"Enough," Judge Hurston declared, and immediately had our attention. "Ms. Clarke makes a point. Now, don't get all excited over there, Annabelle, we're not going to tar and feather him. If you think you can teach him to respect our community, then I'm happy to task you with that."

"Wait...what?" Annabelle's hand fluttered to her chest.

"I rule that Connell MacDhuibh pay all costs associated with restoring the...Oliver statue, as well as perform six weeks of community service to be served under your supervision, Ms. Clarke. Put him to work in the clerk's office or on the reserve project; it's up to you." He slammed his gavel. "We're adjourned."

He got up and left without any further comments, leaving us all staring at one another with a mix of horror and confusion.

"Community service," I heard Langley say on her phone as she walked out of the room, no doubt filling Asher Silas— the owner of the Reapers—in on what had just gone down.

"I'll get the reparations set up," Gregory said, picking up his briefcase. "Damn small-town judges. I guess the good news is you can knock it out before the season starts, which I'm sure is what Silas is going to demand."

"Right," I muttered, trying to understand what the hell just happened.

Gregory and Carson walked out together, leaving Annabelle and me alone.

"Why on earth should I have to supervise you?" she muttered.

I stood slowly, choosing my words with care.

"You know, lass, while I may have imagined you fucking me, I hadn't exactly imagined you fucking me *over*." I adjusted my sleeves again.

"I...I didn't mean for you to be with *me*. I have entirely too much to get done to babysit you." Her chin rose a good two inches as I walked around the table, coming to a stop directly in front of her. Her chin rose even higher, trying to maintain eye contact.

"Trust me, I'm not a child you have to sit." My chest tightened in absolute frustration.

"Well, maybe you'll learn how to take something seriously for once." She arched a dark brow.

"Oh, trust me, lass. Considering you just cost me a summer at home in Scotland, I'll be taking this very seriously. You'll have one hundred percent of my attention." I kept my eyes on hers even though I'd noticed the rapid rise and fall of those incredible breasts.

"Well...okay then. I guess I'll see you tomorrow?" She swallowed. "City Hall, nine a.m.?"

"Monday," I retorted. "I'll be far too hungover tomorrow." I turned and walked out of the courtroom before I said or did anything else that I'd regret.

First off, I was going to have to call my mother, which was easily the worst part of this entire sentence. The woman was going to be sore with me.

But more importantly, this was going to be a damned disaster. I was too attracted to the lass not to say something about it eventually, and I was known for getting exactly what I wanted. And her eyes? Her body language? I'd have bet all of that nine million that she wanted me, too. Problem was that neither of us could stand the other, and it wasn't like I was a relationship guy, anyway.

This was going to be bad. So, so, so bloody bad.

An entire summer spent with Annabelle Clarke would end in one of two ways—homicide or heartbreak, and honestly, I think I preferred the first.

2

ANNABELLE

"*I* thought City Hall would be more...official-looking," Connell's voice sounded behind me, and I whirled from my desk, playfully glaring at my assistant for not announcing the Scotsman's arrival.

"Mr. MacDhuibh is here," Lacy said, all too late.

"Thank you, Lacy," I said as she hurried back to her desk and focused intently on her computer screen.

"What do you mean?" I asked Connell, composing myself as I scanned him from head to toe. The man had worn a tight white T-shirt and Reaper athletic pants—he may as well have been a walking ad for wild sex, and that smirk on his face? Sweet mercy, it promised hours of side-splitting laughter after a proper roll in the sheets.

He glanced around the building, his blue eyes trailing over the polished marble floors, the ancient sandstone walls adorned with framed blueprints and city plans from when Sweet Water was just an idea in the founders' minds. He finished his appraisal by eyeing my assistant's and my desks behind us, the rich maple wood sitting atop more marble, the room free of office equipment save our computers—we kept the copiers and records and such in a closed room as to not mar the beauty of the old building.

"I expected more people, for one," he said. "And definitely more *officey* stuff. Not a museum."

I bit my bottom lip to keep from chuckling. *"Officey?"* I asked. "Is that a Scottish term?"

He tilted his head, his eyes now raking the length of my body. It took everything I had not to smooth the pink Chanel skirt and white blouse I'd picked out this morning. His stare was like a sizzling brand as he took in the curves of my hips, the fullness of my bust, and he lingered on the pink lipstick I'd selected to match the skirt.

"It is," he finally answered. "Now, what duties am I to perform for ye today?"

A warm chill raced down my spine at the way his tongue curled around the words. Damn accent. Why did it make my knees wobble?

I straightened my spine, tearing my eyes off the defined chest I could easily see through his white T-shirt and hustled to the supply closet down the hall from my office. "Here," I said, shoving a bundle of fabric at him. "You'll need to put this on first."

"Why?" He surveyed the brown jumpsuit like it was a rotten piece of fruit.

"Because," I said. "It marks you for what you are."

Connell took a step closer to me, and the hallway was suddenly very hot and very crowded. I didn't lose his gaze, though. Didn't break. Not for a second. "What am I, Annabelle?"

Heat unfurled in my core at the sound of my name, and I cursed myself for letting the Scotsman have such an effect on me.

"You," I said, slightly breathless. Damn him, he *smelled* carnal—like cedarwood and oakmoss—as if he were some ancient highlander who smelled delicious even drenched in sweat.

"Aye," Connell said, dragging out the word. "Me..."

"You are a..." my tongue twisted, and I sucked in a sharp breath, waving my hands as I clicked by him. "You are the person who damaged a priceless statue and therefore are under my full control for the next six weeks."

I stopped in my office, spinning around to face him.

He was smirking again. "Under your full control doesn't sound that bad."

I pursed my lips and pointed behind him. "The facilities are to the left, third door down. You may change in there. I'll have a list of tasks for you when you return."

"Sure thing, boss," he said, and gave me a mock bow before turning out of my office and down the hall connected to it.

I blew out a breath, my cheeks burning.

This would be the longest six weeks of my life.

Less than five minutes later, Connell rounded the corner, and lucky for me, I was already sitting down. Because sweet tea on a hot day, the man made the ugly brown jumpsuit look so damn *good*.

"Seriously?" I grumbled under my breath, tearing my eyes away from the way he'd tied the top half around his waist, the thick brown pants bunching along his strong abdomen.

"What?"

I shook my head and flung a piece of paper at him. He caught it easily against his chest.

"Mop the floors. Lubricate door hinges..." He cocked an eyebrow at me before continuing to read his list. "Clean the bathrooms. Clean basement which includes organizing back records."

I held my breath, waiting.

For him to protest.

To whine.

To offer me a check in whatever number I wanted to make this all go away.

"All right, then," he said. "Where might I find a mop and bucket, boss?"

I turned in my chair and gaped up at him.

That half-smile shaped his lips *again*.

I pointed toward the hallway connected to my office. "To the right, two doors down. You can get water from the facilities."

He nodded, pocketing the list as he headed the direction I indicated.

Lacy whistled from her desk but kept her eyes trained on her computer. "I may need to call Dan up for a quickie on my lunch break because *y'all* are flinging that sexual tension all over the place."

I scoffed. "Oh please," I said, waving her off. "Do what you want with your husband, but there is absolutely *nothing* flying between Connell and myself."

Lacy sucked her teeth. "I don't know," she said. "Sure as hell seems like it. Hell, *feels* like it. The way he was looking at you? Like you were a snack—"

"Stop," I said, shifting in my seat. "You're seeing things." Because I was most certainly *not* his type. I wasn't a model, not even close. I had curves. My stomach was soft, not toned, and my thighs were thick. I loved my body, but I definitely didn't want to be scrutinized by a celebrity athlete who was used to dating stick figures. Not that I'd looked him up or anything.

"Okay," Lacy said, somewhat softer. "Whatever you say, *boss*," she teased.

TWO HOURS LATER, Lacy had gone on her break, practically

15

sprinting out the door and into her awaiting husband's open arms. Newlyweds.

I hunched over my desk, buried in the plans for my biggest city addition yet.

"What's an ostrich reserve?" Connell's voice made me jump, and I dropped the papers I'd been reading all over the floor.

I hurried to scoop them up, but Connell was faster, already on his knees gathering the loose sheets. My heart thudded rapidly in my chest from the sight of him on his knees before me, those crystal blue eyes glancing up to mine as he handed me the chaotic pile.

I wet my lips and took the papers from him with slightly trembling fingers. "Thank you," I said, and settled the paperwork back on my desk.

"So," he said, eyeing the stack. "What's that?"

I bit my lip, contemplating. My excitement outweighed my logic. "Can you keep a secret?"

He grinned. "I *love* secrets."

I placed my palm on the papers. "I'm in the beginning stages of constructing an ostrich reserve."

"Aye," he said, nodding. "I gathered that much from the text. But what of it?"

"Well, as I'm sure you've gathered from running into our beloved Oliver statue with a four-wheeler, the bird is incredibly important to the town of Sweet Water."

"You don't say!" Connell said sarcastically, winking at me.

I pursed my lips at him. "As I mentioned before," I said. "Ostrich racing used to be *the* tourist attraction here in Sweet Water. It brought in the wealthiest from Charleston and all over South Carolina in the thirties."

"Racing." Connell shoved his hands in his pockets. "On ostriches. I still don't get it."

"Well, yes," I said, ignoring the way his blond hair fell *just so* over his forehead when he moved. "Obviously, I wouldn't want to bring the exact races back—I'm humane, after all. But rescuing ostriches in need has always been a dream of mine, as well as bringing them back to Sweet Water as an attraction."

His eyebrows rose, but he nodded. "Ostriches. Important. Got it." He grinned. "How many have ye got?"

"How many what?"

"Ostriches," he laughed.

"Oh," I said, sighing. "I haven't gotten any yet. I've only just started on the permits and potential properties."

"Well, if you need any help—"

"From you?"

He raised his arms to indicate the lack of anyone else standing in my office. "Why not?"

I shrugged. "Didn't figure you cared much about this community. Hence, the whole reason you've been sentenced to suffer six weeks with me."

He pressed his lips together, a muscle in his jaw ticking.

"No," I said, raising my hand. "Don't misunderstand me," I hurried to say. "I only meant with your career and traveling and everything. You don't have much time to put down roots."

Connell cocked an eyebrow at me. "You don't know much about me at all, sweet Annabelle," he said, and I swallowed hard as he leaned down closer to me. "And until ye do, don't make assumptions." He braced his hands on either armrest of my chair, his nose an inch from mine. "Now, *boss*, where are these records?"

I straightened in my chair before standing, breaking his grasp on the chair. The feel of his body against mine, even for the briefest of moments, burned hotter than a summer Sunday.

"That job will take you the longest, I suspect," I said,

17

smoothing out my blouse as I headed down the hallway and to the set of connected stairs leading to the basement. He followed me down, and I flicked on the light to illuminate the massive space. "It's been seriously neglected," I said, my eyes roaming over the array of holiday decorations, extra tables and chairs, party props, and then the countless boxes of public records. "They date back nearly thirty years," I said. "Court hearings, council meeting minutes, etcetera. I've done my best, but most of my time, and overtime, is used up on current events." I sighed, exhaustion settling in my bones simply *looking* at this mess. "And we've just been waiting for the right man to do the job." I tried to lighten the over-whelming assignment.

Connell chuckled. "And you think I'm that man."

"Yes, I do." I stepped closer to him, arching my neck to meet his eyes. "And I *do* know a little bit about you, Mr. MacDhuibh. If you so much as *think* of pulling a prank here and destroying these records, I will personally see to it that you never set foot in Sweet Water again."

He narrowed his gaze, his eyes churning with...offense? Worry? Regret?

"I didn't mean to harm your beloved statue," he said, his voice low, raspy. "And I'm not trying to argue me way out of the chores you're giving me. You can trust me, Annabelle."

A smile played on my lips at the sincerity in his words, but who was I kidding? I'm sure Connell was well versed in seducing women into believing *anything* that came out of that perfect, Scottish mouth of his.

"Good," I said, clearing my throat. "You're free to go at four." I nearly sprinted up the stairs, gulping down the air outside of the basement that wasn't *drenched* in Connell's scent.

The rest of the afternoon was quiet save for the clicks of my keyboard as I resolved a variety of town matters and the slight rumblings of items as Connell worked in the basement beneath me. Sometimes I'd hear him hum some melody I couldn't recognize, but it had a hauntingly beautiful quality to it. The deep tenor of his voice and the rumble from his chest as he hummed, painted images of rolling green hills and stone castles in my mind. I could almost taste the rain in the air, smell the lush grass, *feel* the ancient stone on my fingertips.

"Boss?"

I jolted at my desk, my eyes snapping open from their daydream state.

"Sweet mercy, Connell," I said, clutching my chest to slow my racing heart. "Tomorrow I believe I'll attach a bell to that jumpsuit."

He laughed, the sound genuine and full and it caressed my skin. "I said your name twice. Were ye napping?"

"No," I snapped, straightening my desk. I spared a glance toward Lacy, who bit back her smile. "I was...just taking a moment to think. What can I do for you?"

He jerked a thumb toward the large clock on the farthest wall in my office. "It's four."

I nodded. "You can go."

"Aye," he said. "You already said that."

"Then what—"

"Do you need a ride to *Scythe*?"

My lips parted, a breath rushing from them. "How did you know I was going to *Scythe* tonight?"

"Everyone is going," he said, shrugging. "Celebrate the start of summer vacation—the offseason."

"Oh, well, I..." I sucked in a sharp breath. "I have a few things to finish up here. Thank you for the offer. I'll drive myself later."

Something like defeat flashed in his eyes, but it was gone in an instant. He nodded, backing out of my office. "See you round, then." He turned his back to me and sauntered out of the building.

"I can't believe you didn't take him up on that offer!" Lacy said the second he was out of earshot.

"I have work to do," I said, returning focus to my computer.

"So! You always have work to do. You rarely stop working."

"Your point?"

"If there was ever a time to *stop* working, it's to take a ride with Connell freaking MacDhuibh!"

I chuckled softly, shaking my head. "Lacy, he's going to be working under me for the next six weeks. Not that there *is* anything there, but even if there was, it would be highly inappropriate to engage in such a relationship with a coworker."

Lacy smacked her hand on her desk, gaping at me. "He's not technically your employee. Not like I am."

"He's still under my charge." I waved her off. "Not another word on the matter, please," I said and winked at her. "You can clock out early if you'd like."

She brightened at that. "Thanks, Annabelle." She squeezed my shoulder as she walked past my desk. "And you know, six weeks isn't that long of a time."

"Meaning?"

She shrugged as she headed toward the exit. "Once he's completed his service you two could—"

"You're impossible!" I laughed. "Go! Have fun tonight. Not everyone is drowning in newlywed lust like you are."

She laughed, shaking her head as she left.

When the quiet settled over my office again, I let out a deep breath, the tension in my shoulders tightening from the workload I had ahead of me.

And before I could stop myself, I started humming.

Connell's song.

* * *

SCYTHE WAS CRAMMED NEARLY wall-to-wall with Reapers, so much so it was almost impossible to squeeze my way to the bar Echo currently hustled behind.

"Annabelle!" she said when she saw me. "Make room," she said, eyeing a couple of Reaper rookies. They hurried off their stools and made their way to the pool tables in the back of the bar.

"You didn't have to do that," I said, taking the seat anyway.

"Of course, I did," she said. "They had their drinks anyway." She shrugged and wiped some stray purple strands off her forehead.

"How are you feeling?" I asked, eyes trailing to her still-flat belly.

"Morning sickness is a real bitch," she said, smoothing a hand over her tummy. "But at least I can choose which shifts I work. Nights aren't nearly as bad."

"You don't have to work at all—"

"Oh no you don't," she cut me off, wagging a finger at me. "Not you too. Sawyer has already brought it up a hundred times."

I raised my hands in defense. "We care about you."

"I know. And I'm not the first woman in the world to get pregnant. I'll work until I feel like I can't anymore. Nothing has changed."

I arched a brow at her.

"Well," she said. "Except for the fact that I can't take shots with my customers anymore." We both laughed at that. "Speaking of," she said. "Do you want a vodka soda or just a soda?"

"Soda and lime, please," I said, rubbing the tight knot on my left shoulder.

"Not one for drinking on a work night, still?" she asked, pouring the drink and sliding it toward me.

"No," I said, sipping the bubbly soda water. "I have an early morning. I'm only here because—"

"There's the boss," Connell's voice cut me off as he pushed his way toward the bar. He eyed Echo. "One more, please." He set an empty glass tumbler on the bar.

Echo smiled, her eyes flashing between the two of us before she got to work on his drink.

"Did you get your work finished?" he asked, his body so close it was an effort not to brush against it with even the simplest of moves.

"No," I said, rubbing that spot on my shoulder again. "I never do, and I don't believe I ever will. There is a never-ending list on my schedule and I've come to the conclusion I won't finish it until I retire."

"Here you go," Echo said, sliding Connell's drink toward him.

"Thanks," he said, then eyed where I was currently massaging myself. "You injure your shoulder?"

I laughed, then quickly dropped my hand. "Not so much," I said, fiddling with the condensation on my glass. "It happens sometimes when I stare at my computer for too long. Always the same spot."

Connell set his drink down, hands poised over my shoulders as he eyed me in question. "May I?"

My lips parted, hesitance tying my tongue.

"I had a small shoulder injury in the minors," he said. "My PT taught me a trick."

I flashed a glance toward Echo, who quickly found customers at the other end of the bar to attend to. "Okay," I said, my cheeks warming at the fact that he'd waited until the approval left my lips before touching me.

And then he *did.*

His hands were warm and strong and somehow knew the *exact* spot that tortured me.

Using his whole hand, not just his thumb, he slid over the knot with a sweet pressure that loosened the muscle with each pass. I immediately relaxed under his touch, unable to prevent the half-sigh, half-moan that escaped my lips as he continued to work at it.

And just as my lids drifted closed and the sounds of the crowded bar faded away—

He released me.

My eyes flew open, and I breathed deep and slow.

"How did you do that?" I asked, flabbergasted. The pain that had plagued me for nearly a week was entirely gone. Nothing but free-flowing circulation and loose muscle now. It made my head spin.

He smirked, scooping up his drink. "Old Scottish magic," he said, wiggling the fingers on his free hand.

I laughed. "Whatever it was," I said, raising my glass to his. "Thank you."

"You're welcome," he said, clinking his glass against mine.

We sat there, sipping our drinks, letting the chatter of the other Reapers fill the space between us. Most were talking about travel preparations for the little time off they had in the summer.

A pang of guilt hit me square in the chest.

Connell wasn't making travel preparations.

He wasn't excited over a trip home to Scotland.

Because of me.

Because of my outrage over the statue.

Because—

Oh, calm down. Just because the man has magic hands doesn't mean he gets out of repaying the community for his rash actions.

I nodded to myself, steeling my heart against the guilt gnawing at it.

"I don't believe it!" Connell's booming voice sounded over all the combined Reaper voices, his eyes locked on Logan Ward and the girl on his arm.

"What?" I asked.

"I've never seen him with a girl. Not ever."

Logan made his way over to us, meeting Connell's high five with gusto. "See you started without us," he said, flashing me a soft smile.

"Couldn't wait forever, Ward," Connell said, his brows raised at the girl.

Logan straightened a bit, motioning to the gorgeous brunette who was nearly as tall as him in the heels she wore. Her make-up was perfectly in place, like those internet tutorials I sometimes tried to duplicate and always utterly failed at. "This is my girlfriend, Blaire," he said. "Blaire, this is Connell MacDhuibh. And Annabelle Clarke, city clerk of Sweet Water."

I smiled back at him, raising my glass to him, shocked that he'd remembered me at all. He'd always been so quiet any time I came around here to visit Echo, but he must've been paying attention instead of sulking in silence like we all assumed.

"Nice to meet you," Blaire said, gently touching Connell's shoulder. She lingered there for a few seconds too long, in my opinion, not that anyone asked. She gave me a sweet smile, then focused on Logan. "Anywhere to sit, babe? These heels are killer!"

He nodded, ushering her off toward the corner of the bar with a few extra round-tops.

"Whew," Connell said, leaning against the bar. "Never thought I'd see the day."

"Maybe he was just waiting for the right person," I offered. "Instead of hopping from bed to bed."

Connell shot me a glare. "Who does that?"

It was my turn to smirk. "Not you, surely."

"I wouldn't exactly call it *hopping*." He tilted his head from side to side. "More like mutual visits where both parties leave completely satisfied."

I laughed so hard I nearly spit out my drink. "Cocky, Scot, aren't you?"

"Not cocky when it's true."

"How can you be so sure?"

He leaned closer to me. "Trust me, I know."

"Do you, though?" I teased. "*Loads* of women are fantastic performers."

His mouth dropped, but his blue eyes danced with amusement. "Why would you say such cruel things?"

"I'm just being real," I said, shrugging. "A majority of men think they hung the moon when it comes to the bedroom, but more often than not, they fall flat."

Connell licked his lips. "Sounds to me like you've been sleeping with the wrong people."

"Or sex is overrated."

He grabbed his chest. "Now you're really trying to kill me."

"What'd she say now?" Echo stopped before us, eyeing me like I was about to get sent to the principal's office.

"What?" I gaped at them both. "Is it so bad to be honest? I mean, if *I* can do it better myself then why waste time—"

"Annabelle!" Echo said, laughing. "Are you recanting the tale of the time I dragged you to *Madame Matrix's Toy Shoppe*?"

My cheeks instantly flamed, my stomach dropping to the floor.

"Oh," Connell said. "*Do* tell."

"No!" I snapped. "Don't you *dare*, Echo Hayes!"

She ignored me. "Well, there was this one time I took Annabelle shopping for some fun little things, and the cashier actually *recognized* her. While she was buying...well, anyway. She got so flustered she ended up dropping the three things she'd gathered and made me sprint out of the store."

I ducked my head, covering my face with my palms. "Echo!" I groaned through my fingers. My heart raced, and I was quite sure the bar was on a tilt. "You know I can't handle public embarrassment!" I said through clenched teeth. "How could you tell that story!"

Echo waved me off. "It's hilarious. And I thought that's what y'all were talking about anyway."

Connell held back his laughter and instead nudged me with his shoulder. "That isn't half as embarrassing as the time ye saw me naked."

A laugh burst from my chest, freeing the mortification from my lungs. "Oh, come on," I said. "You weren't embarrassed. Streaking through Reaper Village like that. You were *so* proud."

"Not true!" He chuckled. "Okay, half true. I am proud. I mean, look at me." He motioned to all his gloriousness. "But I didn't know you were there. I wouldn't have done it if I'd known we had a non-resident on the street."

I pressed my lips together to keep from smiling. "Good to know," I said.

Echo blew me a kiss and returned to help other customers.

Connell leaned closer, lowering his voice. "Now, back to what we were talking about."

I tilted my head, feigning innocence. "I have no idea what you're referring to."

That wicked grin shaped his lips, those lips I couldn't help but stare at.

"All right, Annabelle," he said, his voice coaxing, soothing. "We'll revisit that conversation another time." There was a promise in his tone that shook me to my core. I watched him walk back to where a bunch of his teammates were celebrating, hating that I couldn't tear my eyes from him.

Sex may be overrated in my book, but my body sure as hell seemed to think Connell MacDhuibh could change my mind.

3

CONNELL

*T*he first week wasn't too bad, honestly. I'd never shied away from physical labor, and I got a rise out of knowing Annabelle *couldn't* get a rise out of me.

The second week she tried harder, and even when I hung off the side of the building to remove a bird's nest from the roofline, she didn't get to me. I had been raised on hard work, and if the lass thought this was hard, she had another thing coming.

I may have also faked a fall and scared the shit out of her, but really, that was just for fun.

The third week, we were halfway through my sentence, and she started to run out of things for me to scrub, but there was never a lack of shit to get done. I walked into the office with a dusty box of records from the basement, still sporting the shit-colored jumpsuit. I'd tied the top around my waist and gone with a T-shirt because South Carolina in July was no bloody joke.

"You sure it's in there?" she asked with a worried glance as I set the box down on the empty desk in the corner that had somehow become mine.

"Since I'm the one who refiled all of this two weeks ago, I'd have to say I'm pretty certain. Give me a second here." I took the top off the box and sifted through the papers, and she went back to glaring at her computer screen.

Och, but she looked beautiful today. Her hair was piled up on her head, which only drew my attention to the line of her neck just above the collar of her white, pressed blouse. But it was the skirts that killed me. Today it was a black pencil number with a slit up the back that hugged her hips like a second skin.

My workload may have become physically easier in the last week or two, but keeping my hands to myself was infinitely harder.

"Annabelle, I'm going to take off for lunch, okay?" Lacy asked as her husband walked into the office.

"Sure thing," Annabelle answered without looking up from her screen.

If the way Lacy looked at her husband as they left was any indication, we didn't need to see the two of them for at least an hour.

"Is it just me, or do they go earlier and earlier every day?" I glanced at my phone to make sure I wasn't crazy. It was only eleven.

"They're newlyweds," she answered with a shrug. "Give them a few more months and the lunches will stop, and the headaches will start."

"Och, sometimes I forget how jaded you are." I thumbed through the papers until I found the one I needed.

"Not jaded, just realistic."

I walked over and sat on the corner of her desk, then waited for her to give me her full attention. She flicked her gaze at me a few times, but finally gave in with a sigh about a minute later and turned in her chair so she could fully face me.

"Is this where you assure me that not all men are the same and promise me sweet, sweet pleasure if you could just talk me out of my clothes?" She arched an eyebrow in clear challenge.

Ahhh, so our conversation in the bar had stuck with her.

"Lass, if I talked you out of your clothes, I wouldn't need to promise anything. I'd simply show you. Weak men make promises when it comes to sex. Good men let the orgasms speak for themselves." And I would, over and over again. If I ever got this woman in my bed, she wouldn't leave it until she was too weak to walk, and then she'd stay for the very same reason. It would be a vicious, delicious, satisfying cycle.

Besides, if we spent a month in bed together, maybe this attraction would fizzle out and give me my brain back.

Her lips parted, and heat flared in her eyes before she quickly shuttered them. "Did you find the plat map?"

I openly grinned at her change of subject. "Right here, boss."

She took the map from my hands with a grateful smile. "Thank goodness."

"You can tell the Richardsons that the city already has that easement, which means you can legally build the access road to the reserve." Or she could send me over to the Richardsons, so I could tell them exactly what I thought about their constant harassment.

"Thank you, Connell. I'll forward this over to Carson."

Carson. The city lawyer. The one who was in here every day it seemed. "Do you two have a thing going on?"

"What?" Her eyes shot to mine, wide with surprise. "No. I mean, we're friends and have been since forever, but no."

"Right." Why the hell did I feel instantly better? Oh fuck me, wasn't I acting like a jealous twit? I had zero say in who this woman was romantically involved with.

The skin between her eyebrows puckered as she glanced back at her screen.

"You've got the plat map, so now what's wrong?" I asked.

"The PR company wants way too much money to work on the announcement for the reserve." She shook her head and muttered a curse under her breath.

"How much?" I prodded.

"Too much, and don't you even think about paying for it." Her lips pursed as she shook her head. "Shit. Shit. Shit. I was hoping they'd come down, and we just can't afford it."

"Annabelle, how much is it?" Why wouldn't the woman let me actually help around here?

"Connell, your money can't fix everything! I screwed this up, and now I have to figure it out." She pushed her fingers in at her temples.

"The announcement is supposed to be next week?" I asked, eyeing the professional brochures stacked on her desk. Brochures that featured stock photos of ostriches because the woman had yet to secure her own.

For a bird in need of rescue, they sure were scarce.

"Yeah. That was the earliest they could get the announcement out, and we were really hoping that the announcement would spur partnerships with other wildlife reserves, and now it's all just...fucked up."

If I'd been drinking anything, it would have flown out my nose. "Could you say that again?"

"What? That I screwed up?" She rubbed at her temples.

"*Fucked* up." It was the strongest language I'd heard out of her.

She rolled her eyes. "Fuck. Fuck. Fuck."

"Oh baby, yeah, just like that," I teased, but damn if it didn't turn me on.

She laughed but shook her head. "Ugh. Don't make me laugh right now. I don't deserve to laugh. This is going to be so embarrassing when I have to report to the mayor that I screwed—fucked it up. The whole town will know by morning." She leaned forward and put her head in her hands.

"Annabelle, what's so bad about everyone knowing? It's not your fault that the PR team is a bunch of money-hungry bampots." I reached for the back of her head but stopped myself before I made contact.

"Bampots?" she questioned, her voice muffled by her hands.

"Aye. Idiots." My thoughts started churning, and soon I was grinning like a fool. "So you'd actually benefit from announcing a wee bit earlier?"

"Uh-huh," she answered, still hiding. "Not that it matters. It's going to take at least a week to interview new firms, and no one local had their reach. We really need to get the donations going so we can finish construction."

I moved to stand behind her and looked over her shoulder at the quote on the computer screen. Then I looked up the PR firm on social media and snorted.

"Stop laughing at me," she growled into her hands.

"I'm not," I assured her as I took one of the brochures from the pile. A few seconds later, I took a selfie with it. By the time I was done with the post, Annabelle had lifted her head, but the absolute devastation on her face caught me off guard and twisted something inside my chest. "Hey, now. It's not all that bad."

"No, it really is that bad. This reserve project might sound insane, but it would be a great thing for our little town, and now everyone will know that I set us back *months*. That's how long it's going to take to get everything moving again, and we'll miss the estimated opening date because we won't even have the funds to finish it."

I moved behind her and parked my ass on the small table she kept behind her desk, then pulled her rolling office chair between my thighs. "You're really upset about what people might think, aren't you?" Before she could protest her position, I started massaging her temples. She was so bloody tense.

"Well, yes. Oh...that feels good." Her eyes fluttered shut, and she sighed softly.

"Why?"

"It's hard to explain. But that nightmare some people get about forgetting their homework or being naked at school? I can't even think about it. I just freeze up from absolute mortification at the thought. I don't even watch movies where embarrassing things happen. It's like I'm right there with the character, dying on the screen from public humiliation. I would rather break a bone than suffer through something like that." With each word, her posture softened a little until she relaxed against me, her head resting against my stomach.

"I guess I never thought of it like that," I mused, mostly to keep my brain occupied on what we were talking about and not the feel of her skin beneath my fingers.

"Of course, *you* didn't. You, who pranks the entire Reaper team just to get a laugh."

"I never hurt anyone, lass." Just the insinuation had my hackles bristling.

"Not physically," she chastised but moaned softly as I moved my hands to the nape of her neck and massaged the rigid muscles there.

"Not in the way you're thinking, either," I countered softly. "I don't ever prank someone who can't handle it, or wouldn't want me to. Sure, I like to get the guys laughing, but I'm not that big of an arse."

She relaxed so completely that I held the weight of her head in my hand as I worked her neck with the other. If anyone needed to lighten up a little, it was Annabelle, but neither of my methods for relieving tension would sit well with her.

"For example," my voice dropped. "I would never prank you or cause you embarrassment now that I know that about you. Getting someone—for fun, that is—is all about knowing that person well enough to know what makes them laugh. What makes them tick. It wouldn't be funny for me to see you in pain."

Her eyes opened, and that twisting sensation in my chest transformed to an ache. "So you'll never prank me?"

I smirked. "I won't say that I'll never prank you. That feels too final. But I will say that I'll never do anything that causes you to feel humiliated. There's nothing funny about that."

She drew her lower lip between her teeth, and when she released it, I had to physically stop myself from lowering my mouth to hers so I could taste what she had. Where was my usual restraint? Sure, I fucked my share of women, but I'd never been...desperate for one. That's what this was turning into—desperation. Shit.

Her cell phone pinged on the desk, and Annabelle groaned. "Real life calls, I guess. And don't worry about humiliating me. I've done that myself already. I bet that's the mayor, asking if we've signed the PR contract." She lifted her head and I hated the chill that replaced where the warmth of her skin had been.

"I wouldn't worry about announcing the reserve," I said with a grin as she rolled her chair forward and reached for her cell phone.

"Of course, I'm going to..." She scrolled through an app— my guess was Instagram—and her jaw dropped. Finally, she turned to me with wide eyes. "What did you do?"

"I announced it for you," I answered with a shrug, hopping off the table.

"You...just like that?"

"Just like that," I replied, heading back toward my desk.

"I can't even think of words—holy hell, how many followers do you have?"

"A little over a million." I hefted the box of files into my arms and turned to see her gawking up at me from her seat.

"A...million?"

"You don't have to look so horrified, lass." A grin spread over my face at the expression on hers. I'd finally found a way to stupify Annabelle, and I was savoring every minute of it.

"I'm not, I swear!" She stood quickly as I walked past her desk. "I just didn't realize how popular you are. Of course, I know you play for the NHL and everything, I just didn't realize people cared so much about..." her voice faded as she scrolled through my feed. "Abdominals," she muttered.

"Well, they do make it easier to power through my shots." This was even better than pranking her.

She flushed that deep shade of pink I loved as her eyes flew back to mine. "What? I mean, how do I say thank you?"

"You just did."

The smile she gifted me with felt far more intimate than my last dozen sexual encounters. I got the hell out of that office before I acted on it.

* * *

ONE WEEK LATER, I was two-thirds through completing my sentence—not that I was counting. Fine, so I was counting, but not for the reason I'd initially started the calendar marking at home. In two weeks, I wouldn't have a reason to see Annabelle every day, which sent a stab of unexpected anxiety through my system.

Which was probably why I was back at the office at seven at night, bringing Annabelle dinner.

35

"You're a lifesaver!" she exclaimed as I walked in. "I just took two more calls, both from donors! We're going to be able to fund the completion of construction plus some."

"That's great!" Amazing what having an entire NHL team repost your announcement could do for fundraising.

"Really, I can't thank you enough for picking up dinner. I'm famished."

"Can't have you wasting away," I said as I put takeout from Luigi's, Sweet Water's only Italian restaurant on the lone clean desk in the room—mine.

"Like that's going to happen," she said in a mocking tone.

I caught her gaze, then let mine rake down her body, taking in every curve the sheath dress let show. "Losing even an inch off that arse would be a tragedy."

"Uh-huh." Her cheeks pinkened—which was quickly becoming my favorite shade on her. "Let's get this dished so I can get back to my desk."

"You can't eat at your desk." Her shoulder brushed my arm, and the contact sent a jolt of awareness down my spine just like it did every time we accidentally—or purposefully touched.

"Yes, I can, and I have to." She reached for the bag, but I snatched it up by the handles and lifted it higher than she could reach. "Seriously?"

"You cannot eat at your desk. You live at that thing. You need a break."

She huffed, then jumped a little for the bag. I simply raised my brows and the bag higher.

"What are you? Five?" she growled.

"I'm not lowering this until you agree to take a break."

"I have at least ten more emails to return tonight, not to mention going over the reserve budget one last time before I send it to the mayor's office tomorrow. Now give me my dinner!" She lifted her hand slowly, and I jerked the bag out of reach again just in time.

"As soon as you agree to take a break. It's pretty simple when you think about it, lass."

She glared up at me. "You have no idea how much pressure I have on me right now."

"I've been in this office five days a week for the last month, Annabelle. I'm well aware of everything you have going on. I know you're overworked, which is why I'm doing something about it."

She eyed the bag. "You know what's on my plate, sure, but not the pressure. You make millions of dollars a year playing a game. *A game*, Connell. This is probably the most important thing I'll ever do for my town!"

I ignored her jibe at my chosen career and instead took a step forward. She took one back. "I honestly don't think that's true, but even if it was, then you aren't going to do anyone any good this stressed out."

"I'm not stressed! I'm under pressure! There's a difference!"

"Is there?" I took another step, and she retreated. "You live in this office right now. You're not sleeping enough or eating regularly."

"I have too much to do!" she snapped as we continued our path across the floor. "I have to answer all of these donation questions, meet with the contractors, approve the plans for the observation deck, contact media about the grand opening, and that has nothing to do with every single tiny detail that goes into planning the opening, and did I mention that we don't even have ostriches yet? I can't sit down and eat because my brain won't shut off, you giant...guy!" Her back hit the wall, and I grinned.

"You should really take more time to plan out your insults, lass."

She blinked up at me as if realizing she had nowhere else to go, and I closed the distance between us, bracing my forearm against the wall on her left. "Where...where did you put the food?"

"I left it back on the desk." I shrugged.

"What? Why?"

"Because I'll need both my hands to get your brain to shut off for a minute."

"I have work to—"

I stole the rest of her words with my mouth. Damn, her lips were plump and sweet and too fucking perfect. The simple caress felt like lighting the wick on a stick of dynamite—a tiny lick of heat that would eventually explode if we weren't careful.

My lips brushed over hers once more before I lifted my head slightly. "Head clear yet?"

Her brown eyes widened, and my stomach tightened at the haze of desire I saw there. "Not yet," she whispered, her gaze dropping to my lips.

Hers parted.

I took them. My fingers tunneled through the hair at the nape of her neck as I claimed her mouth, sweeping inside to taste her. Fuck, she was sweet and tasted like the apricot tea she loved.

Her soft little moan was even sweeter. Fingernails bit into my back, and I growled. The strength of the need that hit me shook my control, but I still couldn't stop myself from kissing her over and over, taking her mouth with deep strokes and teasing licks.

She was heady, intoxicating, and if I kept this up, I'd be addicted with only this one kiss.

I moved my forearm from the wall, sliding my hand behind her back and pulling her against me. Damn it, she felt even better against me than I'd imagined. Her soft curves cradled the sharp lines of my body as I leaned into her. This was a woman who could take all of me—no holding back, no keeping myself in check.

She kissed me with the kind of abandon that spoke to her desire. She was pure want and need. No artifice. No coy smile and practiced flirtation like every other woman who'd come onto me after signing that first contract.

Fuck, I was never going to stop. I'd kiss her until we both died with the need of it. Until the flames licking their way down my spine and hardening my cock consumed us both.

"Annabelle," I groaned and sank back into her mouth, the kiss turning openly carnal as I took her mouth with the same rhythm that I rolled my hips against hers.

She whimpered and tilted her head so I could kiss her deeper, and I took complete advantage of what she offered. I'd take everything this woman offered.

I felt her gasp all the way in my dick when I set my lips to her neck. How did she smell so fucking good? Everything about this was so good—

"Stop!" she squeaked.

I lifted my mouth from her skin and sucked in a breath, praying she didn't just—

"Connell, you have to stop. *We* have to stop." Her voice shook, and so did my hands as I untangled them from her delicious body.

My heart raced faster than it did while I was on the ice, and the struggle to control my breathing was so real it would be embarrassing if I cared about hiding my reaction from her. But I didn't. I wanted her to see what she did to me.

"Annabelle." The plea was obvious as I stepped back, giving her the space she demanded.

"We can't do this." She pushed at my chest, and I stepped back. "This..." she gestured between us, "can't happen. Not while you're working here. Or ever, really." She pushed again, and I pivoted, backing away.

"Annabelle."

"Don't. Don't you say my name like that, all soft and burred and accented. That's not fair!" She shook her finger at me before pushing me back again. "I mean, we can't do this, right? Right. It's wrong! And it's an abuse of power."

"Lass, I didn't mean to make you feel powerless." Another step back.

"What? No, *I'm* the one in power, remember? Right. I'm the boss, and you're the employee. Kind of. Right. Either way, this is wrong, and we can't do it. I mean kissing, not *it*, you know. And we definitely can't do *it*, either!" With every statement, she pushed, and I retreated. "It doesn't matter that you kiss like a romance novel, and you're built like... well, you are. This." Step. "Isn't." Step. "Happening."

I found myself in the hallway outside the office.

"Annabelle—"

"I'm so glad you agree. Good talk!" She slammed the door in my face.

What the bloody hell just happened? I raised my fist to knock on the door, but instead, I lowered it and shook my head. I'd never been one to pressure a woman who'd said she didn't want me, and I wasn't about to start with the one woman I wanted above all others.

"Right. Good talk." I gave the door a mock salute and headed down the hall.

I was halfway home before I realized she hadn't just stolen every ounce of my control—she'd taken my dinner too.

4

ANNABELLE

*C*onnell's lips against mine, his strong, hard body pressing into me. Sweet tea on a hot day, the memory *haunted* my every waking thought.

I was no virgin, but I'd never, not *once*, felt something as powerful and intoxicating as his kiss.

And it was *just* a kiss.

But his tongue had moved expertly against mine, his hands gentle yet demanding on my body in the most delicious way. I'd felt safe and wild, and my head had damn near exploded.

Until I'd come to my senses.

Damn my senses.

I sucked in a slow breath, rubbing my forehead as I sat at my desk. I'd been trying to make sense of a simple spreadsheet for an hour, but all I could see or taste or *feel* was Connell. I practically purred between my thighs, the ache a true and harsh craving for something I'd never experienced before. Something electric.

But it could *never* happen again.

I was his superior. He was basically my employee. The scandal!

My pulse spiked as my mind played his kiss on repeat in red hot flashes.

Those lips.

That tongue.

His scent making my head spin.

Where did he *learn* to do that? Make a woman completely forget where she was, *who* she was. I'd never been so reckless in my life.

And I liked it.

It had been one of the single most freeing moments of my life…

And it was just a kiss. I couldn't *imagine* what he'd do to me if I gave in.

Oh, wait, yes, I could.

I'd wait until after dark, *long* after I'd locked up City Hall. Then I'd wait until Connell finished up his work. Of course, he'd stop by my desk. He always did. And he'd ask me if he could walk me to my car, like usual, but I'd shake my head, my entire body trembling with nerves. I'd bite my lip, gather some courage, and motion for him with a sexy, come-hither look, like in the movies. Then I'd arch against my desk as he stalked to me…no *prowled* to me. And he wouldn't hesitate to snake his arms around my waist and haul me against him. He wouldn't think twice about kissing my neck, teasing the spots I had there, and going lower. *So* low he'd drop to his knees, run his hands up my thighs and under my skirt. He'd smirk up at me, his eyes sparking with wicked delight to find I hadn't worn panties today. And then he'd gently, tenderly plant kisses on my thighs and up and up until he reached the very center of me. The feel of his mouth on me, so slick and hot, I'd have to grip his blond hair to keep from falling over. To keep from screaming as he tongued me—

"Falling asleep on the job, boss?" Connell's voice clanged through my daydream, and I jolted so hard I bumped my knee against my desk.

I rubbed my bare knee while spinning in my chair, glaring up at the man. "Remember that bell we spoke about?" I said through clenched teeth.

He pursed his lips but crouched to examine my knee.

A stuttered breath escaped my lips at the sight.

Damn this man straight to hell.

"It doesn't look so bad," he said, daring enough to slide his hand over the red spot.

I trembled from his touch, from the confident look in those stunning blue eyes.

"You all right?" he asked, still smoothing his fingers over the affected area. "You look flushed."

I parted my lips, then shook my head.

"What were ye thinking about?" He flashed me that wicked grin of his, that playful smirk that promised trouble and laughter and ecstasy. And apparently, the one I couldn't resist because there I was, smiling back at him.

"Wouldn't you like to know," I said, a bit childish, but I couldn't very well tell him where my head had just been now could I? Or rather, where *his* head had just been. Lord save me, I could still feel the heat between my thighs from the fantasy.

"Aye," he said, his hand pausing his inspection of my knee and now simply resting there.

I swallowed hard, forcing away the electric sparks buzzing across my skin from his touch. I cleared my throat and scooted back in my chair, his hand falling off my knee and onto his own.

"Did you need something?" I asked, my tone breathless.

He cocked a brow at me. "You *know* what I need," he said, and the words sizzled down my spine.

I lifted my chin slightly. "You need me to say thank you again for using your amazing social media status to announce the reserve? Or do you need me to explain the organization process again?"

He shook his head, some of the blond strands falling across his forehead as he stood up. I followed his gaze but remained seated. "Not exactly what I had in mind."

"That can't happen again," I said in a hushed tone, thankful Lacy had already left for the day. "I'm your boss, as you so fondly call me. It isn't ethical." There, I'd regained some of my common sense. "What happened...it was a mistake."

He grinned again, leaning down closer to me. "A mistake, eh? Is that why you've been showing up to work wearing all these mouthwatering pencil skirts and silk blouses?" His eyes trailed the length of my body, my bare legs peeking out of the red skirt I'd selected for today, over the white V-neck blouse that showed a dignified amount of my cleavage.

I wet my lips, my mouth suddenly dry from the heat in his gaze. "I...I don't know what you're talking about," I said, flustered. I hadn't thought he'd noticed my change in work attire, but I couldn't help it. If the man was going to saunter around my place of business looking like a snack, then by God, so was I.

"Oh, I think you know exactly what I'm talking about, Annabelle."

A warm shiver skittered across my skin at the way his tongue shaped my name.

"I think you know more than you let on," he said. "And I think you know this thing between us..." He motioned from me to him. "Is impossible to deny."

Heat flared in my chest, up my neck, under my cheeks. How could he be so brazen? So bold to say exactly what was on his mind?

"I'm not denying it," I admitted on a whisper. "But I'm not indulging it either." I waved a hand between us. "This can't happen. I'm your—"

"Boss," he cut me off, then smiled. "But not for long," he added. "I can wait." He winked and then pointed to the computer behind me. "How's the ostrich hunt going?"

I blinked a few times, my head spinning from the jump in topics. He seemed to notice the whiplash and laughed softly. I straightened in my seat, shifting gears. "Not as well as I'd hoped," I said. "There aren't as many ostriches in need of rescue as I assumed there would be. At this rate the reserve will be completed before I secure the birds. They're incredibly expensive and, thanks to you, we do have a considerable budget but I'm trying to figure out if there is any other option so we can save funds for advertising and stocking the reserve. So…I'm at a crossroads. For now."

"I'm sure you'll figure it out."

"Oh, I know I will. I just need time to puzzle it all out."

Connell glanced at the clock. "You have plans tonight?"

I pressed my lips together. "Connell we can't—"

"Eat?" He cut me off. "I'm having dinner with Logan and his girlfriend. Come with us. Help me not be a third wheel."

I bit my lip, contemplating. I *was* hungry, but doing *anything* with Connell outside of this office seemed dangerous.

"It's just food, Annabelle," he said. "No expectations or schemes." He held up his hand in an *I swear* motion.

A thrill rushed through me. The only dinner plans I'd had for tonight consisted of a cold sandwich and a good book.

"Okay," I said. "Where should I meet you?"

"I'll text you the address," he said, slowly backing out of my office. "See you in a bit."

And before I could argue, the damn Scot was out the door.

* * *

"Baby, just show them!" Blaire teasingly nudged Logan in the booth seat across from us.

I'd cringed when the waitress had guided us to a booth instead of a table, knowing I'd have to sit so close to Connell. Have to feel the warmth of his body and smell that intoxicating scent all night. I'd silently cursed *and* thanked the waitress as I'd slid in, taking the interior seat, as had Blaire.

"They don't need to see it," Logan said, his voice strong but quiet, calm.

"Babe!" Blaire shook her head, her long hair swishing over her shoulders with the move. Her playful laugh did nothing to mar the perfection of her makeup, either. It only made her look more beautiful.

I shifted in the booth, suddenly wondering if I'd selected the correct dress tonight. A vintage Dior off-shoulder dress, it hugged my curves on the top and billowed out in the skirts, stopping just below my knee. When I'd slipped it on, I'd felt as beautiful as the queen Marilyn Monroe herself, but next to Blaire? God, there wasn't an ounce of fat on her, that much was clear from the skin-tight tube-top black sequined dress she wore. She looked *perfect* next to Logan. Like she belonged there.

She'd look perfect next to Connell too, or anyone like her. Much more than myself.

Stop.

Right. I sucked in a sharp breath and straightened in my seat. I loved my body. I loved my life. I'd never questioned it before, and I wasn't about to start questioning it just because of one mind-blowing kiss from Connell. We weren't an item, so I didn't have to worry about being compared to girls like Blaire.

"Here," she said, plucking her phone from the corner of

the table where she'd had it all night. She'd managed to snap four selfies, five different angles of her meal, and even went as far as taking a picture of our after-dinner coffees. "Check this out," she said and turned the screen to face us.

Her Instagram feed filled the screen, but she expertly clicked an image from the dozen shown and enlarged the post.

"That's your gear bag," Connell said, tilting his head at Logan.

I too was confused as to how this was the career-impacting post she'd been talking about for the last half-hour.

"Yeah," Logan said.

Blaire rolled her eyes. "I made sure he laid his favorite Under Armor shirt over the top," she said, smiling at Logan. "It got over twenty-thousand likes, and now they've contacted him for a sponsorship!"

"Congratulations," I said, grinning at Logan. "That is wonderful."

Logan wrapped his arm around Blaire. "I've never under-stood social media, much. Mostly my PA handles the page, but lately, Blaire has been taking lead," he said.

"I've tripled his followers," she said, leaning into him. "And this Under Armor deal will be the first of many, babe."

Logan shrugged but placed a tender kiss on her forehead.

"That's nice, man," Connell said before taking a sip of his coffee.

"Thanks," Logan said. "Good for me, good press for the team. I'll take it."

"You'd have a hundred more offers rolling in if you'd just model like I've been asking," Blair said.

I couldn't argue there. Logan had rich brown eyes, dark hair, and was just quiet enough to be marked as the broody and mysterious type women lost their minds over. He also had a Reaper body, which meant sculpted perfection. Though he was beautiful, nothing stirred inside me when appreciating him. Not like it did when Connell...*breathed*.

"No," Logan said, his tone a bit sharper than before. "I won't."

"He will," Blaire said, ignoring Logan and instead looking directly at Connell and myself.

"I've told you a hundred times, Blaire," he said. "I'll never model."

"Tons of your teammates do it. Tons of celebrity athletes do it." She rolled her eyes again. "Use what you have—"

"No."

Connell and I picked up our coffee mugs at the same time, glancing at each other through the awkward tension. I pressed my lips together to keep from laughing at the wide-eyed look Connell flashed me.

"Okay," Blaire said, finally focusing on the severe look Logan wore. "Sorry, babe." She stroked his chest. "I didn't mean to bring it up," she continued. "I'm just so proud of you for your deal."

The tightness in Logan's shoulders visually loosened, and I watched, fascinated at the way Blaire coaxed him back to his previous pleasant state.

"That didn't get awkward at all, did it?" Connell asked me an hour later as he walked me to my car outside the restaurant. The couple of interest had already left.

I laughed softly. "Not at all."

We stopped outside my closed drivers' side door, the warm night air carrying the scent of the rose bushes decorating the exterior of the building.

"Do you know why he's so against using his good looks for publicity?" I asked, curious.

Connell leaned an arm against my car. "So you think Ward's attractive, do you?"

I grinned. "Anyone on the planet would think he's attractive, Connell."

A muscle in his jaw ticked, but there was a playful mischief in his eyes as he stepped closer. "You say such awful things," he said, his body so close to mine his knees brushed the billowing skirt of my dress.

"He's not my type," I said, my heart racing as I held that gaze.

"That's better," he said. "And who might be your type?"

I bit my lip. "Definitely someone serious," I teased. "Someone truly grounded. Not a goofball. Absolutely not an athlete."

Connell leaned down, his breath warm on my cheeks. "Sounds boring."

I gaped at him in faux-shock. "Then *I* must be boring."

He shook his head, and I hated how much I wanted to push back those strands of blond hair from his forehead. "You're far from boring, Annabelle."

I lifted my chin. "Oh, yeah? Then who do you think is my type?"

He smirked, his eyes trailing down my face, my neck, and up again. "Someone who can make you laugh. Push you out of those confined boundaries you keep yourself in. Someone who can let you be your powerful, professional self during the day, but the minute you come home? He takes over. Takes care of you. Lets you lose that control you cling to in favor of complete, mind-blowing, *freedom*."

My bottom lip trembled from the tight breath that loosed from my chest at his words. Heat snaked through my blood, pulsing in my core with an endless hunger.

Kiss him.

Wrap your arms around his neck and drag him into your car.

Invite him home.

"Good night, Annabelle," he said before I could say one coherent word.

I breathed a sigh of relief at him saving me from something I knew I'd regret. And maybe he'd sensed that. Maybe he knew me better than I thought. Because I couldn't...*we* couldn't...and he understood that. Respected it, and damn him for it because it made me like him even more.

"Good night, Connell," I said as he headed toward his car across the lot. "Thank you for dinner," I called just as I'd slipped opened my car door.

He spun around to walk backward, his dark blue suit shaping his body like it had been made for him. "Of course," he said, and winked at me. "See you tomorrow."

I bit back my smile and hurried to sink behind the wheel and close the door, scolding myself for already counting down the hours until tomorrow came.

5

CONNELL

"So, you're really not coming?" Cannon asked through the speakers of my Jag as I pulled onto a country road just outside Sweet Water. He was the best defenseman on the Reapers. Hell, he was probably the best defenseman in the NHL. He was also covered in tats from head to toe, had an infamous temper, and was scary as fuck to the general population.

Lucky for me, I was not the general population.

"I can't. I have a work thing," I told him, watching the GPS carefully so I didn't miss her house. Not that there were many houses out here.

"Right. So not sure if you remember, but skating *is* your work thing."

"And I would love to get on the ice with you again today, but I told Annabelle I would go to her family barbecue." We'd just had a pick-up game yesterday.

After a good thirty seconds of silence, I sighed.

"What do you want to say, Cannon?"

"Nothing. I didn't realize you two were that close. Or that

you were *family-meeting* close with any woman. Or any man. You know I don't care how you swing."

"Ha. Funny. And it's not like that. I guess her family has been asking to meet me since we've been working together for five weeks now." One more week, and I'd be done with my community service.

"Ah, she wants to show off the prize pony. Got it. What I don't get is why you agreed to it."

"Because…" I blew out a frustrated sigh. "Because I want her."

"Then fuck her and move on like you usually do."

"It's not that simple." The truth of that statement had my hands strangling the wheel as I passed the first house since turning onto this backroad. Damn, where the hell did this woman live?

"You don't just want her. You like her."

"Yes, and I have no bloody clue what to do about it. There, is that what you were asking?" A line of parked cars appeared up ahead on the right.

"Not—"

"She's impossible. You know that, right? She obeys every rule and does everything by the book. That's why she's so against going on an actual date with me."

"Because you're a convicted criminal serving his sentence under her? Or because she thinks that all you want is to get her under *you*?" he asked, a trace of amusement in his tone.

"The first," I admitted since the way she'd kissed me back last week implied that the second might not be an issue. "We're polar opposites. The woman seriously needs to loosen up."

I pulled up behind the last car and parked, counting at least seven other cars. Exactly how big was her family?

"Look, Scot, I'm happy to play Dr. Phil, but I'm the last person you want to get relationship advice from. I've yet to find a woman I'd like to fuck more than once or twice. But it's funny because both Noble and McCoy are probably who you'd want to talk to about relationship shit, and ironically, they're headed to the rink to skate right now."

He left the hint hanging there in the air.

"Yeah, yeah. You guys have fun."

"See ya." He hung up without waiting for me to say goodbye because that's just what he did.

I grabbed the box of cupcakes I'd brought from Sweet Treats, the local bakery, and mentally patted myself on the back for getting two dozen instead of one. By the time I reached the front porch of Annabelle's house, my short-sleeve button-down was threatening to stick to my skin from the heat and humidity.

The porch was decorated with boxes of cascading flowers in pinks and purples and even had a porch swing. It was exactly as I'd pictured it—not one flower petal out of place.

Before I could knock, the front door was yanked open by a woman with a wide grin. "You must be Connell," she said in the same deep southern drawl Annabelle used.

"I am," I answered with a practiced smile.

"Well, come on in!"

"Thank you."

She pushed open the screen door, then led me in. "I'm Annabelle's Aunt Milly. Belly-Boo? Your very handsome Scotsman is here!" She called out as she looked me up and down. "And that accent? My, my!"

We walked through a well-kept living room and turned the corner where the floorplan opened up to the den, kitchen, and dining room. Holy shite, there were a lot of people here.

"Aunt Milly, I've told you a million times not to call me that," Annabelle chastised with a tight smile as she pushed through the small crowd. Her cheeks flushed, and I immediately got it—she was embarrassed.

"I brought ye cupcakes," I told her as we met beside the dining room table.

"Oh my Lord, did you hear him talk?" a feminine voice asked from the kitchen.

Annabelle grimaced.

"Dinna fash yerself, lass," I said softly. When she arched an eyebrow in confusion, I laughed. "Sorry. I mean, don't worry. I'm used to being gawked at, remember?"

"It really means a lot that you'd do this," she whispered as she reached for the bakery box. Her hair was down today, the curls braided down one side of her face until they stopped just above her breast. I nearly swallowed my tongue when I saw the way her retro wrap dress hugged her frame. It was pale pink, which I figured had to be her favorite color by now.

"If it means I get to spend time with ye, I'm in. Now introduce me to your family, Annabelle." The urge to touch her was overwhelming, and my hand rested against her lower back as she turned to face her family.

Every single set of eyes was on me.

"James! Pat! Get in here!" Milly called out the back door.

Usually this was when I'd crack a joke, but I knew it was important to Annabelle that I not act like...well, me.

Two men came in through the sliding glass door and removed their hats, which must have been Annabelle's cue because she took a deep breath.

"Now that we're all here, I'll only have to do this once. Everyone, this is Connell MacDhuibh. Connell, this is...well, it's everyone."

They all waved.

"Pleasure to meet ye," I said with a nod.

"Connell, we've heard so much about you!" A woman in

54

her fifties smiled as she came over, and I couldn't help but echo it because it was Annabelle's.

"Ye must be her mother."

The woman startled with surprise, but quickly recovered. "Yes! I'm Tara. We've heard so much about you from our little Belly—Well, our Annabelle. Now let me take these off your hands, dearest."

The cupcake box disappeared from Annabelle's hands, and we were swept into a flurry of family. Names flew left and right, and I did my best to remember everyone, but that lass didn't have a family, she had a *clan*.

It must have taken the better part of a half-hour to get through everyone, but Annabelle stuck to my side until it was dinner time, and then she took the seat next to mine.

"Now, the Clarkes have been in Sweet Water since about a decade after it was founded," her father, Davis, told us as we passed the barbecued chicken around one of the long tables that had been constructed in Annabelle's dining room. Good thing the lass kept folding tables in her storage room because I'd counted and there were twenty-two of us here.

"And we've lived here ever since," Aunt Milly added as she passed another dish to the right.

"Not Uncle Grady," Taylor, Annabelle's eight-year-old niece, argued. "He moved to New York."

"God save his soul," Grandma Mary muttered at the end of the table.

"My brother works on Wall Street," Annabelle whispered while the others were distracted.

"And that puts his soul at risk?" I asked, tilting my head toward hers only slightly. If I turned even an inch, my lips would graze her cheek.

"Anything above the Mason-Dixon line puts his soul at risk," she whispered.

"Och. Well then, I guess that explains it."

We grinned at each other until Tara cleared her throat from across the table. "So, Connell, tell us how you like our little town?"

"I quite like it," I assured her. "It's nice to live somewhere I don't have to worry about the press or paparazzi. Miami was a wee bit too much for me." I took the potato salad from Taylor, then held it so she could dish some for herself.

"Need help, darlin'?" Jackson, her dad, asked from her other side.

"Nope. I can do it myself."

"I'm here!" a bright voice announced from the doorway. A woman with straight brown hair beamed as she walked in. Her sundress looked tailored, and her heels were high.

"It's about time!" Tara answered with a bright smile. "I left a seat open next to me. Go put your things down and get over here, Savannah."

I glanced at Annabelle in question only to find that she was already watching me. Appraising my reaction? And why had she gone all tense?

"You okay, lass?" I asked quietly.

"My older sister," she said in way of explanation. "We're about a year apart."

"Good lord, Belle, who did you bring to dinner? He's about as—my stars and garters! Are you Connell MacD-huibh?" Her eyes flew wide, and her hand rose to her throat.

"I am," I answered with a smile. From what I knew about sisters, I needed to make a good impression on this one to stand a chance with Annabelle. "And you must be Annabelle's sister."

"Sure am." She gave me a wide, polished smile and then tilted her head at Annabelle. "Why didn't I know you were bringing a guest? I would have rescheduled the showing of the Carley place!"

"Your job is important," Annabelle answered with a shrug, but I noticed her smile was real.

"Hardly," Savannah countered. "I certainly don't need to be showing houses on a Sunday if you have a friend over." Her eyes narrowed slightly in a way that suggested Annabelle hadn't heard the last of the question, but she deflected, anyway. "Jackson, pass the chicken."

"So what is your family like, Connell?" Annabelle's dad asked.

"Not quite as big as this one." There was a rumble of laughter around us, and Annabelle's lips lifted in a soft smile. "Growing up, it was just me and my mother, so it was quiet. Guess I made up for that by spending most of my time in a noisy hockey rink."

Annabelle's eyes flickered in surprise, and then her shoulders fell. "I kept you from your mother."

"No," I assured her. "*I* kept me from my mother. Besides, she remarried when I was nineteen, and Callum already had three kids, so trust me, she's not lonely."

She nodded, but there was still something a bit more reserved about her.

"Savannah, are you judging the Miss Sweet Water contest again this year?" Milly asked from down the table, which gave me the opportunity to eat.

"I think so," Savannah answered. "It's better than letting Mr. Oliver pretend he's judging while really he's just staring at those girls in their swimwear. That man has got to retire."

"Our Savannah was Miss Sweet Water three years in a row!" Tara exclaimed. "Of course, you can't compete once you're twenty-one, so then she started judging."

My brow puckered in confusion. The town had an official *Miss*?

"It's a beauty pageant," Annabelle explained between bites.

"Girls answer questions, dress up, show off a talent. It's a competition."

"Not that you'd know anything about that, would you, Belly-Boo?" a guy teased from the second table in the dining room.

Annabelle turned to stone, and I twisted in my seat to see who had hurt her feelings, but her hand gripped my thigh, stopping me cold.

"Don't call her that, Uncle Holt. You know she doesn't like it," Savannah snapped, then sighed as she turned back to face Annabelle. "Besides, Belle was busy at college, remember? Acing all her classes from what I remember."

"Figures you'd have straight A's," I teased.

"And a color-coded planner," she quipped, but her smile was fake. I fucking hated it. Annabelle was beautiful no matter what, but she was exquisite when she let her real emotions show—both happiness and anger.

"Our Annabelle was always the smartest in her class!" Tara boasted with pride.

"I'm sure she was." I laced my fingers over hers on my thigh and ate with my left hand as dinner fell into a rhythm of questions. I received my fair share about hockey, and the others on my team—mostly from Cash, Annabelle's nephew, but I was relieved that the conversation didn't revolve around me.

They all checked in on one another. How was Savannah's real estate business doing? How was the veterinary clinic where Jackson worked? Were the kids excited to get back to school? It was all so...normal.

Eventually, Annabelle relaxed next to me, and even when she took her hand off my thigh, she shifted in her seat so her knee brushed mine. She was just as active in the questions, asking how her dad's fields were doing on their hobby farm and if her mother was going to help train any of the pageant girls this year.

We finished up, and I was promptly kicked out of the kitchen when I tried to help with the dishes, so I joined in with the small army who tore down the extra tables and put them away.

I showed Cash and Taylor a few magic tricks to keep them busy and earned more than a few giggles for my effort.

"No one at school is going to believe that we had dinner with you," Cash lamented in the way only thirteen-year-old boys can.

"Well, how about I get ye some tickets to a game this season?"

"Really?" His eyes grew wide as saucers.

"Absolutely. I'll make sure to let your Aunt Annabelle know when."

Cupcakes in hand, the kids took off with their father, and the rest soon filed out, until only Savannah and Annabelle's parents remained in the house.

"It was so nice to meet you, Connell," Savannah acknowledge with a nod and then moved in to hug her sister where we stood in the kitchen. "You owe me details," she whispered.

I almost grinned but stuffed the rest of my cupcake in my mouth to hide it.

Savannah waved and walked out.

Annabelle watched me carefully, and I swallowed the last bit of the lemon and raspberry deliciousness.

"You survived," Davis said with a slap to my back.

"Aye," I agreed as Annabelle peeled the wrapper from her cupcake as it sat on the counter.

"Brave of you to take us all on at once. And yes, I know you two are...what was it, dear?" Davis asked, his silver brows nearly meeting as his forehead crinkled.

"Just friends," Tara answered, sliding a bowl of grapes in

front of Annabelle and nudging her cupcake down the counter. "Isn't that what you said, Belle?"

What the fuck just happened?

"Yep! Just friends." She smiled at her mother, then her father, but her knuckles were white where she gripped the counter.

"At least for the next week," I teased. Her eyes flew to mine with a shake of her head, but she stopped strangling the counter.

"Oh. Okay, then," her mother drawled slowly, looking between us. "Davis, why don't we get out of here and leave these two to...whatever they have planned for the night."

Her father took the cue, and after hugging Annabelle and shaking my hand, the two departed.

Annabelle popped one of the grapes in her mouth, and I watched, utterly transfixed as her lips closed over it. Fuck, that mouth was going to get me into trouble.

"Thank you for doing this," she said, staring at the grapes.

"Ye already said that," I reminded her. "Now what's the deal with your sister?"

Her gaze snapped to mine, and it wasn't friendly. "Why do you ask?"

The granite counters were cool against my back as I leaned against it so I could watch her. "Because the minute she walked in, ye turned to a statue, but I can tell ye love her."

"I do," she answered defensively. "Savannah is one of my best friends. She taught me all about makeup and dresses and boys. She really is the perfect sister." Her eyes flickered toward the peeled cupcake, and I pushed it toward her. "She means well," she whispered, and I knew she wasn't talking about her sister.

"That's a question for another time. Why were you so uncomfortable when she got here if you think she's perfect?"

Annabelle lifted the cupcake and took a bite.

Damn, I wanted to taste those lips.

"Because you were here," she answered after a moment.

"I don't follow." Her sister had seemed protective of Annabelle, not predatory.

"You wouldn't." She scoffed and rolled her eyes. "She's perfect. Beautiful face, beautiful body, beautiful heart."

"So are ye."

The woman glared at me.

"What? Ye are."

"I'm pretty," she admitted. "And I try my best to be a good person. To make things better for other people. But I'm no Savannah. She's a damned beauty queen! When you think of the epitome of the American standard of beauty, Savannah is it. No, don't look at me like that. You asked, and I'm answering. I've always been...thicker than my sister, and I'm good with it. I love my body. I love my life—"

"I happen to love your body, too," I assured her, letting my eyes wander to the rise of her breasts at her neckline.

"Shush." She wagged a finger at me. "I love my sister. I'd die for her. But I've never brought home a boy who didn't take one look at her and think they were with the wrong Clarke sister, and just the thought that you might look at her like they did had me as nervous as a cat in a room full of rocking chairs."

"I don't even know where to start with that statement." She thought I'd want her *sister*?

"You don't start with it." Her voice dripped sass as she took another bite of her cupcake.

"Lass, those boys were idiots, thank God."

She looked at me like I was the daft one and swallowed her cupcake. "What?"

I took the cupcake from her hand and put it on the counter, only because I wanted her full fucking attention. Then I pivoted until I stood in front of her and pressed her back against the counter. "They. Were. Daft. And I'm so bloody thankful because if one of them had realized what a treasure ye are, I wouldn't be here with ye."

"Don't," she whispered, but she didn't shy away. No, the lass lifted her chin and stared me down.

"I don't want your sister." I gripped her hips and groaned as her flesh filled my hands. "I don't want any other woman, and that's actually a problem for me right now because this body? It's all I see when I close my eyes at night."

Her lips parted and she rested her hands on my chest, but they didn't push me away.

"Fuck, Annabelle, you have me twisted in knots, and all we've ever done is kiss." I rubbed my lips over hers but didn't kiss her.

She gripped my shirt and tugged me closer. "I'm not your type."

"Fuck that. You are *exactly* my type. Soft and curved and so fucking sexy that I'm permanently hard when you're near."

"What?" She arched for a kiss, but I held my lips just above hers, not giving in to what either of us clearly wanted.

"You heard me." I pulled her against my erection. "Feel that? Now tell me again that you're not my type. You Americans have such a fucked up idea of what a woman should look like—should feel like." I gripped her arse, and she gasped as I lifted her easily, placing her on the counter.

"What should a woman feel like?" she asked, her breaths coming faster.

I cupped her face between my hands and let my thumbs graze over her skin. "Soft, with silky skin just like this." I passed over her lips and almost forgot what I was doing when she kissed the pad of my thumb. "Lips made for kissing, just like these."

I lowered my head and passed my lips over hers, letting

my tongue catch the sweet aftertaste of frosting on her lower lip.

"Connell," she pled, tilting her head for my kiss, but I didn't give it to her. Instead, I retreated, only to run my hands down her neck and then the sides of her ribs.

"Fuck, Annabelle, ye have the most perfect breasts. I don't even need to undress you to know it." She arched, and I took the invitation, cupping the overflowing mounds in my hands. "Damn. *This*. This is exactly what a woman should feel like. One day I'm going to taste these. I'm going to see if your nipples are as pink as the dresses you love, and then I'm going to suck them into tight little points until you're begging for more."

She whimpered and rolled her hips against mine.

Fuck, I wasn't going to make it.

Yes, you will. For her.

"A woman feels like a road curving through lush hills, taking you to hidden places. A woman demands your attention just like that road because you don't want to miss one dip or hollow." I stroked my hands over the dip of her waist, and then I gripped her hips and pulled her to the edge of the counter.

"Connell," she begged again, her voice pitching higher as her hands slammed to the counter behind her in an attempt to keep her balance and control.

Control was the one thing I wasn't going to let my high-strung Annabelle have.

"A woman has hips a man can grab ahold of. Hips that can take every thrust and give back just as much as she's willing to take." Just the thought of thrusting inside her tight heat had my cock throbbing behind my zipper.

I placed my hands on her bare knees and met her lust-filled gaze with one of my own. When she shifted her legs

63

slightly, widening for me, I let out a growl of pure, primal appreciation.

Then I sent my hands under her dress and was met with skin softer than satin as I moved to her thighs. "A woman has thighs strong enough to wrap around a man's hips. Thighs thick enough to cushion her man as he fucks her to mindless pleasure. Thighs that—" I groaned as I reached her inner thighs. "Feel just like this. God, Annabelle, do you know what I would give to feel you wrapped around me?"

"I might have an idea," she admitted between quick breaths.

"Good. Because God, lass. You are exactly my idea of a perfect woman." My thumbs ran lightly over the edge of panties that felt like lace. Just picturing her had my dick straining at the zipper. How long had it been since I'd wanted a woman like this and not taken her?

Fuck that. How long had it been since I'd wanted a woman like this, period? Had I ever? Annabelle had me so tightly strung that I'd snap if I wasn't careful.

My thumbs traced the edge of her panties again, and she rocked her hips, urging me on.

"Connell, I'm on fire." She sat up straight and gripped my shirt in her hands. Then she started flicking the buttons free one at a time, baring my skin.

"Lass," I warned.

"Please?" She looked at me with those eyes, and I would have given her whatever she asked for. My life. My career. Anything.

"Do with me what you will," I said with a grin.

She tugged her lower lip between her straight, even teeth, and made quick work of removing my shirt. As soon as it was off, I sent my hands straight back to the heat of her, only inches away from her core even though she remained fully dressed.

But if she kept looking at me like I was dessert, she wouldn't be fully dressed for long. "What are you thinking?" I asked as her gaze raked over me with the same hunger I felt.

Her fingers traced the lines of my muscles, running over my pecs, then tracing down my abs. "I think…" Her eyes met mine. "I think I could probably come just from looking at you."

My cock pulsed, firmly in agreement.

"That's exactly how I feel about you," I told her. Then I moved my thumb over slightly and groaned at the feel of her through the lace that covered her pussy, wet and so warm.

She gasped and gripped my neck, pulling me to her mouth.

"Let me touch you," I begged, uncaring that I hadn't begged a woman for anything since…ever.

Her breaths hit my lips in ragged bursts, and I was nearly undone. Fuck me, I hadn't even really kissed the lass tonight —had barely touched her, and I was teetering on the edge of losing my control.

"Annabelle." Was her name a plea? A warning? I didn't know or care.

She arched her hips, pressing my hand harder against her heat. "Do with me what you will," she whispered.

I was smiling when I crashed my mouth to hers. There was no sweet seduction or coaxing this time. I took her mouth like I owned it, laying siege to every sweet inch and demanding her surrender. Fuck, she tasted like raspberry icing and Annabelle.

With each sweep of my tongue, I sank further into her, losing myself in her taste and texture, her need fueled mine until I thought we'd both go up in flames. When I retreated, she followed, licking into my mouth like she owned *me.*

Maybe she did.

Nothing compared to kissing Annabelle. I was ruined for any other woman.

Her hips rocked against my hand, demanding friction. A simple move of my fingers and I was beneath her panties—her *thong*. God, I wanted to see that beautiful arse...just not tonight. She'd regret it in the morning, and I'd hate myself for making her feel that way.

"Fuck, woman. You're soaked for me, aren't ye?" I slipped my fingers through her wet folds, already slick and slippery.

"Yes," she admitted, pulling me back to her mouth.

I kissed her lightly, tasting each gasp and whimper as I ran my fingers from her opening to her clit. When I circled the swollen bud, she cried out and pushed harder against me.

"You're so responsive. Do you know how good it's going to be the first time I fuck you? The second time? Every time? God, Annabelle, you're right there for me, aren't ye?"

She moaned when I rubbed her clit. "Please, Connell. *Please.*"

"Aye, love. I have you." I slid one finger inside her and nearly lost my fucking mind when her body gripped me tight.

"Yes!" She rocked again, riding that finger, and I slipped a second one in, stretching her taut flesh.

"That's it. Take what you want," I growled into her neck. I worked her clit with my thumb as I fucked her with my fingers, wishing it was my cock.

Her muscles locked around me and her breaths came closer and closer together. "More," she demanded, and I brought my mouth to hers as I pressed her harder, worked my fingers deeper. "God. Yes. Yes, Connell!"

She screamed my name as she came on my hand, and I watched with wonder as her eyes flew wide, then fluttered shut. I stroked her as she convulsed around me again, her body riding out the aftershocks of her pleasure.

When she sagged against me, I made myself pull my hands from her. I sucked in one breath after another, willing my control back in place. Slipping those panties to the side so I could take her with my cock wasn't an option. Not tonight.

Instead, I kissed her softly.

"Ye are so fucking perfect, Annabelle."

Then I stepped back, thanked God that my keys were still in my pocket and retreated.

"Connell?" she asked, all soft and welcoming.

"I'm leaving, lass. I have to. If I don't walk out that door right now, I'll fuck you on that counter. That's how far gone I am for ye."

She blinked rapidly as her brow puckered. "Okay?"

"I know ye better than you think I do. You'll regret it in the morning. So I'm leaving. I have a week left of my service, and you can follow all the damned rules ye like. Once that week is over, you'd better be ready, because I'll be servicing *ye*."

Her lips parted, and before she could say something that would fuck over all my good intentions, I walked out of her house.

Without my shirt.

My hands shook the entire drive home.

6

ANNABELLE

*S*aturday mornings were the only mornings I allowed myself to sleep past seven—a simple luxury I looked forward to each week.

I slipped my white cotton robe over my green silk shorts pajama set and poured myself a generous cup of coffee. The early morning sun shot golden rays through my kitchen window, illuminating the counters in a relaxing glow.

A warm shiver raced down my spine, the red-hot memory of Connell's hands sliding up my skirts, his fingers coaxing my body to the edge of pleasure, his kiss pushing me over with sweet tendrils of ecstasy. I blew out a breath, heat pooling between my thighs at just the thought.

Then my heart swelled—he'd left. For me. Because he *knew* me. Knew I'd been ready to invite him into my bed and that I'd regret it. Because he still worked for me, and I wouldn't dare be accused of taking advantage of him. And yet, he'd made me shatter for him with the mere use of his fingers. *He* truly held the power.

Taking a steadying breath, I settled at my kitchen table, today's paper open and ready for devouring. Work far from my mind, my muscles relaxed as I sank into my routine. Normally, I'd dive straight into the local news section, but lord help me, I fanned through the pages right to the sports section. I sighed, shoulders sinking—the feature story centered around Reaper Cannon Price and how he'd cooled his bad-boy antics for over two weeks, a feat in the press's opinion.

It's not that I'd *wanted* the press to intrude on Connell's life, but I couldn't help my desire for...*more*.

And more is what he'd given me at my barbecue.

A warmth fluttered in my core again, and I couldn't *stop* thinking about his hands, his lips, his smell. Sweet mercy, I wanted to drown in that man.

We'd kept our distance for the last six days as the construction finished up on the bare bones of the reserve, but I couldn't tell if it was out of a sense of self-preservation, or if he'd had the regrets he'd tried to save me from having.

Don't go down this road.

Right.

We weren't in a relationship or...any type of ship, really. Besides, he was an NHL star. Traveled more than he stayed put. Pranked more than he took things seriously. And he...

Made me feel alive.

Awake.

Desired and vibrant and I'd never laughed like I did with him.

He's temporary.

True. I knew Connell's interest in me was a temporary thing, a curiosity he wanted to satisfy before returning to his one and only true love—hockey. And I couldn't blame him. I loved my job as well, had found it to be my passion in life. I never knew another living soul could match that passion, set it ablaze, and burn brighter than the sun, though. Not like Connell had.

I took another sip of my coffee, letting the hot liquid soothe my mind of its churning.

A low, deep cooing-like sound hummed from my backyard, stopping me mid-second-sip.

I set down my mug, pushing back from the table, my brow furrowed. Had an animal gotten trapped in my yard again? Last summer, I had the unfortunate experience of finding a large skunk pacing the lining of my fence—clearly, the poor creature had forgotten how he'd managed to get *into* my yard in order to get *out* of it again. Luckily, I knew the best humane animal control man in Sweet Water, who came in minutes to handle it.

I grabbed my cell from the kitchen counter on the way to my back patio, just in case I had to make the same call again.

Again, that deep, nearly muted *cooing* sounded as I slid open my sliding glass door and stepped onto my back patio.

My phone slipped from my grasp, clattering against the navy-blue rug covering my patio.

"What in the world?" I gasped as I stared at not one or two but *four* fully grown ostriches.

In. My. Back. Yard.

Two of them had to be at least seven feet tall, the other two not far behind. Each was gorgeous in its own right, their black feathers inky in the morning sun.

But...they were in my *backyard*.

I slowly knelt, scooping up my phone. I skipped my humane animal guy's number and dialed the one and only number that would make sense of this...situation.

"Morning," Connell answered after one ring. "I thought I might be hearing from—"

"Get. Over. Here. *Now*," I whispered into the phone, my heart racing as I watched the giant creatures strut this way and that, mere feet away from me.

"I'm already almost there," he said, a laugh in his tone. "I thought you said you sleep in on Saturdays?"

"I do," I whispered. "I did."

"Seven-thirty is sleeping in to you?"

"Connell MacDhuibh," I whisper-hissed.

"Oh no," he said, and I could hear a car rumbling down my street. "Full name? I'm in trouble."

"You have no idea."

"I'm here." The line went dead, but I heard a car door open and shut.

The sound triggered one of the larger ostriches because he went from mildly strutting to full out running.

At *me*.

I yelped and dashed out of the way just before he would've plowed me over. Squealing, I kept running the second I realized he wasn't the least bit deterred by my attempt at escape.

The other three ruffled their feathers, but remained huddled in the corner of my backyard, near where my marigolds were in full bloom.

The grass was cold and wet against my bare feet, the morning's condensation doing nothing to help me gain traction. Desperately, I tried to circle back, hoping to zoom back inside my house to safety, but the damn bird was clever and blocked my every attempt. All the while he rumbled that odd, throaty sound and fluffed his feathers at me.

Laughter echoed in the distance, and I spared a glance to find Connell outside my fence, his phone pointed at me.

"Connell!" I yelled, dodging the bird by only an inch.

"Uh oh," he said, pocketing his phone at the clear desperation in my voice.

He hopped the fence in one leap, made it t0 me in a few strides, and then...

I was over his shoulder.

And we were back over the fence in no time flat.

Connell shifted me until he cradled me against his chest, his muscled arms warm against the bare skin of my legs. I clutched his neck, breathing rapidly from the chase.

"You all right?" he asked after I hadn't made a move to unbury my face from his neck.

I finally pulled back, sighing as I realized the bird *hadn't* followed us over the fence. He'd gone back to his strutting as if he already owned the entirety of my backyard. I wiggled against Connell, and he immediately set me on my feet.

I shoved against his hard chest, but the motion barely phased him.

"If you ever, *ever* post that video anywhere, I will *kill* you."

Connell grinned. "I wouldn't dream of it," he said. "I know you hate to be embarrassed."

"Embarrassed?" I snapped. "I was terrified!"

He pursed his lips in a faux-pout. "I thought you'd be excited."

I raised my brows.

"I bought them for you...for your reserve." He motioned to the exotic birds.

The tension in my shoulders dropped, and my lips parted as my heart swelled. "You *bought* them." Adult ostriches were insanely expensive. Like... purchase a car expensive.

He nodded.

I opened and shut my mouth several times.

"Why?"

He stepped closer to me, tucking a strand of my hair behind my ear. "It's important to you."

I glared up at him, gently punching his hard stomach. "This doesn't get you out of your community hours, you know. You still have four days."

A deep, glorious laugh tumbled from his lips, the sound so delicious, so infectious. I had to join in.

"I honestly thought I'd beat you over here," he said. "I never dreamed you'd wake up so early on your day off. Forgive me?" he asked, the picture of pure innocence on his face.

I glanced back at the gorgeous birds, finally realizing what their presence meant.

My reserve would happen.

I'd bring back the glory of the ostrich to Sweet Water, with Connell's help.

I turned back to him and smiled before throwing my arms around his neck.

Connell caught me easily, my feet hovering off the ground.

"Thank you, thank you, thank you!" I squeezed him hard, happy tears coating my eyes. "You have no idea how much this means to me."

His arms held me to him, his mouth at my ear. "I have a feeling I do."

I relaxed my hold on him, leaning back enough to meet his gaze, a weight in my chest. "I'll never be able to repay you for this," I said, the feeling sinking like a stone in my stomach. I wouldn't. Ever. Never in my lifetime would I make enough money to pay him back. Just another vast difference in the lives we led.

He cocked an eyebrow at me, a chiding look in his eyes. "This is a gift," he said. "An investment, actually. In the town I live in."

I smiled softly.

"Someone told me that bringing these birds back would put Sweet Water on the map again, and since I'm a loyal citizen of Sweet Water, I'll be damned if I don't do my part."

I melted. Completely. Entirely. *Melted.*

He continued to hold me there, no hint of him wanting to

let me go as I stared into those mischievous, wonderful blue eyes.

That rumbling sound happened again behind us, louder and longer this time.

"What…are they doing?" Connell asked and turned us so I could see.

One of the larger birds was making the sound and flapping his wings in wave-like motions while one of the smaller birds bobbed its head up and down while kneeling on the ground.

My mouth dropped.

"Sweet tea on a hot day, Connell," I said, eyes snapping back to Connell's. "Did you get *breeding* birds?"

Connell sucked his teeth. "Eh, the breeder I purchased them from might've said something about a female in heat."

I gaped at him, then at the birds, and back to him.

"Sorry?" He flashed me an honestly apologetic look. "I can call him back, see if we can—"

A laugh burst from my chest, cutting off his words.

Connell joined me, setting me back on my feet.

"They're perfect," I said once I could breathe again. "Now come on," I said, motioning for him to follow me around to the front of my house.

"Inviting me in, are you?" He asked, trailing behind me.

"Not like that," I said, a slight tease in my voice as I ushered him inside. "You and I have to find a corn supplier fast."

"Corn?"

"Can't have my birds starving, now can we?" I grinned at him.

"No, we can't have that," he said, his eyes trailing my short cotton robe as he followed me into the kitchen.

"Right," I said, eyeing my lazy morning attire. "You get to Googling," I said, situating him at my kitchen table. "Help yourself to coffee. I'll go change." I spun on my bare feet, prepared to bolt upstairs, but Connell gently caught my wrist, stopping me.

"I think you look perfect," he said, and I swear my heart leaped for him, for the honesty in his words, his eyes.

I stood there, highly contemplating jumping the man right then and there in my kitchen, but I heard that deep cooing outside and came right back to reality. "I'll be right back," I said, flashing him a look of deep thanks.

He released me, winked, and then fished out his cell, fingers flying.

Once inside the safety of my room, I debated taking an ice-cold shower before getting dressed. Because sweet *mercy* Connell was doing everything in his power to set every inch of me on fire.

And I'd never felt a burn so sweet.

7

CONNELL

J ran a towel over my hair then threw it into the laundry basket on my way downstairs. As a Thursday night in the offseason went, it was all pretty normal. Workout done. Shower done. All there was left to do was make myself something to eat and relax.

But it wasn't really a typical Thursday, seeing that I'd finished my community service hours today. With the Saturday I'd put in about four weeks back, I'd completed all six weeks, and now I was...what? Free? It was the weirdest feeling, as though I'd adjusted to a normal life and a normal job in the short six weeks it had taken me to work off the ire of Sweet Water.

Well, that and the eleven-thousand-dollar check it had taken to repair the pedestal and carve the names of the first race winners back into it.

Last week, I would have been showering for a whole other reason. I would have been on my way to Annabelle's to ask her out for real. But she'd avoided me at all costs this week, going so far as leaving me a list of tasks to work on every day and then making herself scarce. She was either embarrassed over what had happened in her kitchen or pissed for the same reason. But that didn't add up to the small smiles she'd give me when we ran into each other at the reserve, so I was at a complete loss.

It wasn't like I had a lot of experience pursuing a woman.

The hardwood was cool but not cold on my bare feet as I came down the stairs and headed for the kitchen. Nothing was cold in August down here.

The doorbell rang, and I changed mid-course, turning to answer it. I was fully prepared to tell Logan that I didn't want to hang out with him and his social media savvy girlfriend as I opened the heavy door, but it wasn't Logan.

It was Annabelle, holding a frosted cake on a crystal cake stand.

Her hair fell in a riot of dark curls down her shoulders, and she wore a white sundress that showed off just how much her skin loved the sun. Her lips were glossed pink, and her eyes were locked on mine with almost an air of...panic?

"What's wrong?" I asked.

"Nothing? Why?" She tilted her head in question.

"Because ye look like you did after Arnie chased you across your yard. Like you're not quite over the scare." Not that I would have been either. That wee beastie took us three hours to get him out of her yard so we could transport him to the reserve.

"Oh, really? Sorry. And you know Arnie didn't mean to scare me. He was just having fun." A corner of her mouth lifted.

"Right. Ye should have named him Lucifer. I have that video if ye need to be reminded of his lack of manners."

Pink crept up her cheeks. "Sweet merciful heavens, no. I never want to see that video! Delete it already!"

That was never going to happen. Mostly because she'd

had an incredible smile before Arnie had decided to chase her out. "So then what has you flustered, lass?"

"Well, to start with, this cake is kind of heavy." She nodded toward the confection.

"Och, sorry. My manners are as bad as Arnie's. Give that over and get in here." I took the cake from her and stepped back so she could come in.

"Thank you," she muttered as she stepped through the threshold, already glancing about my house.

"I'm the one to say thank ye. Ye brought me a cake?" I walked past her, taking the bit of sugar to the kitchen.

"I made it," she answered, her eyes darting this way and that as she looked over the pictures that lined my walls.

"Ye made it?" I looked at it with a whole new appreciation as I set it carefully on the gray granite counter.

"Yep. It's lemon and raspberry. Nothing big, just something I whipped up after work." She leaned forward, examining a picture.

"Lass, it's only eight o'clock. You made that in three hours?" What other hidden talents did the woman have?

"It only took about two," she said with a shrug. "Is this your mom?"

I joined her at the wall that ran the length of the hall from the entry to the family room and took a closer look at which picture she'd taken an interest in.

"Aye," I answered with a smile. "That's the summer before I graduated college." The summer we'd taken a few weeks in the highlands so I could get to know my new siblings.

"She's beautiful."

"She is."

"Everyone is so...happy," she mused as she walked down the hall with slow steps, looking at all the pictures.

"Well, I wasn't going to hang pictures of sad friends." I laughed, and she rolled her eyes.

"I'm not sure you have sad friends. It's like you either attract happy people or you make the people around you happy." She paused at another photo. "When is this?"

"Last fall. It was our first month of practice." I grinned at the shot, where Axel was full cringe as a bucket of ice water fell on him from where I'd set it on the locker room door. Lukas, Logan, Hudson, and Nathan were all open mouth in shock and laughter. Even Cannon had deigned to smirk. "It was the first time I felt like I'd found a team where I belonged. Not that I didn't love Miami, but we were a team of skaters there. Here, we're more like a family."

"Wasn't he mad at you?"

"Axel? No. He cursed at me and then got me back with itching powder in my pads. Fucker ruined about five hundred bucks in gear, but damn if it wasn't funny—looking back, of course." I shrugged.

"Have you always been like this?" she gestured down the wall of smiling, laughing faces.

"With the pranks?"

She nodded, moving down the wall.

"Gods, no. My mother would have killed me if I ever pranked her. But I spent a lot of time making her laugh. My dad leaving was really hard on her, and so I felt like if she was laughing, she couldn't be sad. But she's really happy now, and I'm glad for it. She deserves it."

She looked up at me with an appraising look but didn't speak.

"So ye made me a cake?" I inquired, caught between trying to figure out why she was here and simply being happy that she was.

"Oh, yes!" Her smile was fast and bright. "I meant to give you a little send-off at the office, but we got all caught up taking those pictures at the reserve, and by the time I got back, you were gone. And of course, you *should* have been gone. It was five o'clock. So I went home and baked."

"That was sweet of ye." She was sweet. All of her.

"You did a lot more than you signed up for. And I almost added a ball and chain—you know the jail type, not the married type—but I wasn't sure you'd appreciate that."

I laughed. "Just knowing you thought of it is enough."

"You know, this is probably the most traditional house on the block," she said as she peeked around the corner at the formal living room that I never used. "I don't know why I expected you to have one of the modern ones, but this one is actually my favorite."

"Is it?"

"I walked around all of the floor plans while they were being built. I'm the one who set up all the covenants so Mr. Silas would feel comfortable building here." She touched a puck that sat on the entry hall table and then looked at me quizzically.

"Of course, you designed the rules," I teased. "That's my first game puck from when I was nine years old."

"Really?" She looked at it again.

"Yeah. I keep it to remind me just how damned lucky I am to be here. That this is the dream of every nine-year-old boy on skates, and I can't take it for granted."

"I never thought of it that way," she murmured. "You're all so confident—cocky even. It's hard to think of you as little boys with big dreams." She looked up the staircase that led to the second floor.

"Would you like a tour now that the house is complete, Annabelle?"

She seemed to think about it for a moment and then nodded. "I would."

I led her up the stairs. "I chose it for the porch. I really liked the porch. It has four bedrooms upstairs and a guest-house in the back, which I thought Mom might like if she comes to visit with Callum."

"What do you do with the other bedrooms?" she asked as we passed the first guest room.

"I have a giant bounce house set up in one, a ball pit in the other, and—" I tried my best, but I burst into laughter when her jaw dropped. "Och, Annabelle. They're guest rooms."

She scoffed and shook her head in obvious relief that I wasn't that immature.

"Besides, I keep the bounce house in the basement," I told her over my shoulder as I walked into my bedroom. "And this is my room."

She took in the massive, sturdy furniture and calming blue tones I'd had it decorated in. "And how many women have taken this...tour?" Her tone was relaxed as her hand ran across the dark blue comforter, but there was a tension I didn't like.

"Quite a few, I imagine."

Her eyes flew to mine.

"I know Bailey, Gage's wife, looked at this house first. And of course Langley and Echo wanted to see it when I threw a party a couple of months ago. Faith and Harper have been up here, too." I crossed my arms over my chest and waited for her to understand.

"That's not what I mean." She arched an eyebrow at me.

"I know what ye meant. I'm not going to tell you that I haven't been with women, because I have, but the number is probably less than you imagine and more than I wish. But none of them have been in my home."

"Really." She gave me a look I couldn't interpret, and then made her way to the giant windows that lined one of the walls.

"Really. You don't bring the crazy puck-bunnies home,

81

lass. That's a rookie mistake. And honestly, it's been a while since I've been with a woman."

"How long is a while? Because I have a feeling that we have two very different definitions of the term." She turned to face me, and that same panic was in her eyes.

"I haven't had a relationship in a couple of years, and I haven't slept with a woman for months. Since May." I crossed the floor but kept enough distance between us that she wouldn't feel trapped.

"Since May? But you guys won the Stanley Cup in June." Her forehead crinkled.

"Aye, but I saw ye for the first time in May."

Her lips parted. "And that...you...but…"

"You're cute when you're flustered." I took the final steps between us and tucked an errant curl behind the shell of her ear. "I saw you in the street that day with those big sunglasses and wee heels—the tiny ones, and all that glorious hair in waves. After that, there was no one who appealed to me quite like you did—you do."

"You were naked," she blurted out, pink staining her cheeks.

"Aye."

Her eyes locked with mine, and tension flooded the room. She'd seen me naked. I'd had my fingers inside her last week, and we were standing in the middle of my bedroom.

She swallowed and spun toward the windows, ruffling the skirt of her dress with the quick movement. "Is that a waterslide?"

I grinned, coming to stand beside her. "Aye. Fun, isn't it? Plus, I had them put in wee water features—they call it a splash pad—for when we have Reaper barbecues. Honestly, I just like the slide."

She sputtered a laugh. "Just when I think you might actually be a grownup."

"If I ever truly grow up, I'm dead. Life is too short to live it all stuffed up inside someone else's box of rules, Annabelle." I watched her carefully, catching the nuances of her expression as she absorbed what I said.

"My last relationship ended when I graduated college a couple of years ago," she said suddenly, fisting her hands in the material of her dress. "He wanted to live in Atlanta, and I wanted to come home, but he'd insisted—begged actually—that I try long distance. So we did. And it seemed to work fine, I didn't miss his...physical comfort all that much, and the phone conversations seemed like enough to bridge between visits." She took a deep breath, her cheeks flushing. "Then, I decided to surprise him one weekend. I hopped a flight in one of my best dresses and headed toward his apartment. Only, I spotted him sitting at an outside table at this cute little restaurant right next to his building. He had flowers lying across the table—my favorite kind—and he was laughing at something the woman sitting across from him said." She stared at the floor as she continued. "And I was so excited to see him there, so pleased with my bold plans to surprise him, that I rushed right up to him, hugged him and kissed him quickly."

I cringed for her.

"Right," she said, catching the look. "You know what was happening. But I didn't. And once I realized I'd walked in on a date..." She buried her face in her hands. "I was mortified. You know how well I handle that." She shook her head. "And I promised myself then and there that I'd never put myself in that position again. To be blindsided like that. Publicly humiliated. It's not worth it." She sighed. "And I couldn't have truly loved him because I didn't really miss him when it was over. Maybe I missed the possibility of him, but that's not the same."

"No, it's not," I said softly.

"He wasn't my first or anything. I've been with a few men," she admitted as she looked out over my backyard.

"As is your right." Not that I didn't want to hunt down each of those men and cut their hands off for having touched her. The primal instinct was absurd, but it was there.

"I've never had a one-night stand or anything. I've had feelings—friendship or otherwise—for every man I've brought to my bed." Her hands flexed in her skirt again.

"I wouldn't think less of you for any choice you've made—"

"No, you don't get it." She turned toward me. "None of them were like...you."

"Scottish?" I teased.

She arched a brow. "None of them were professional athletes—"

"Well, we're kind of rare. Except around here. Jesus, there are professional athletes all up and down this street—"

"Connell!" she snapped, but there was a lift to her lips. "Be serious for a moment."

"I'm always serious when it comes to you," I said softly. When I reached for her, she stepped back.

"I like the predictable guys. The ones with five-year plans and sensible shoes. The ones who follow the rules. I like my men safe and dependable, and—"

"Boring," I interjected.

"Sure, if that's what you call it." She folded her arms under her breasts, pushing the creamy globes to the neckline of her dress.

Every intention I'd had not to think about getting my mouth on her flew out the window.

"You... you are none of those things. You're wild and unpredictable, and you couldn't care less about rules. You're downright reckless, which is completely and utterly terrifying because you might be reckless with *me*."

My entire body tensed, but I kept my mouth shut, waiting for her to say her piece.

"And there's part of me that doesn't even care, which is even scarier! I have my life in perfect order, and then you run out of your house—naked—with the most incredible body I've ever seen and these eyes that melt me like butter on a warm muffin, and this accent. God, your accent really isn't fair! And you're funny and a little irreverent, to be honest, but you make me feel *alive*."

"And this is a bad thing?" I asked slowly, still hung up on the fact that she liked my body and my eyes. Sure, the body was a tool for my career, but I'd never been so willing to use it as a weapon to break down a woman's defenses before. I'd never had to.

"It's a very bad thing because you go back to being a hotshot NHL star in a couple of weeks, and I'll still be Annabelle Clarke, city clerk for Sweet Water. You have the power to completely turn my life upside down, and you already have!"

"Lass, I've never stopped being an NHL star, and I'm quite mad over the city clerk of Sweet Water. That all sounds pretty perfect to me." Trying to keep my hands off her, I went to stick my hands in my pockets only to realize my sweatpants didn't have them. *Smooth.*

"God, won't you listen to what I'm saying? No, you just stand there in your T-shirt that I want to yank off and those sweatpants that aren't hiding much, let me tell you. And you're so *you* that I'm a puddle before you even touch me. Do you have any idea how much I want you?" If there wasn't so much turmoil in her eyes, I would have laughed.

"I have a pretty good idea because I'm in the same boat." I'd been living on the edge of need and madness for weeks.

"Oh no. I have it *bad.* I dream about you. I fantasize about you while I'm in the shower. I daydream about your hands

85

and your mouth, and the way you kiss. I couldn't even be around you this week because I was afraid I'd jump you in the middle of the office right in front of Lacy! I don't do this! I don't do crazy, wild lust and irresponsible choices, and that's *all* I want to do—make wild, lustful, crazy, irresponsible choices with you."

My cock was hard as the wood of my headboard before she was finished. That same wild lust she described clawed through my veins, demanding appeasement. I wanted this woman more than I wanted my next meal. She *was* my next meal.

"Aren't you going to say anything?" She had the nerve to pop out one of her hips and glare up at me.

"I was waiting until you finished." Each of my breaths were measured as I fought to keep my feet right where they were.

"Oh." Her lips formed that perfect little shape and stayed parted.

"Are you finished?"

"Um…yes. I think so." She tugged her lower lip between her teeth, and I nearly growled.

"Good. Because I'm going to count to three. And once I reach three, I'm going to carry ye to my bed, strip ye naked, and fuck ye until we're both come so many times that we're too exhausted to move. That's how badly I want ye, Annabelle. Do you understand?"

She blinked a few times but finally nodded. "I understand."

"Good. Ye want rules? I don't have them. Ye want calm and boring? Then ye need to walk out that door because I want ye too badly to make myself leave. I might not be the safe choice, but I can promise that you'll always be safe with me. Annabelle, I'm serious. If you don't want this—if you don't want me inside that beautiful body, then you *have* to walk away."

"I understand," she whispered, her arms falling to her sides.

"One." I stripped off my shirt and threw it. She licked her lips.

"Two." My sweatpants went the same direction, leaving me nude as the first time she saw me. Her eyes widened, and her breath left in a little huff as she looked her fill. There was no fear in her eyes when she finally brought them to meet mine.

"Three."

I waited a heartbeat, then two.

Then she was in my arms, her mouth on mine in a desperate kiss. Our tongues tangled and rubbed as we gave up fighting this attraction, and simply gave in.

I lifted her into my arms and carried her to my bed, kissing her the entire time. Her fingers tangled in my hair as she took control, claiming everything she wanted. Thank God she wanted *me*.

Once I had her in the middle of my bed, I took off her heels and then started kissing my way up her legs as she fought with the fabric above.

I had just licked a particularly sensitive spot on her inner thigh when she cursed. Loudly.

"Annabelle?" I asked as I looked up, leaving her dress bunched around her middle and exposing a pale pink thong that had my mouth watering.

"I'm stuck," she admitted with a grimace as she fought with her dress. "I can't get the damned thing off because I'm laying on it."

"I bet I can get if off...and ye." I grinned and came up on my knees, then helped her to sit up. "If ye ever need help getting naked, I'm your man."

"Ha." She rolled her eyes but lifted her arms with a smile. I slowly pulled the fabric over her head, until she was left in nothing but that thong and a matching, strapless bra.

"Fuck," I hissed as I laid her back on the bed. "God, the plans I have for ye."

"Oh really?" she teased, squirming beneath me.

"Aye. Really." I kissed her with abandon until she rocked underneath me, pressing her soft skin against my cock.

I savored every gasp and studied every moan as I kissed my way down her body. But when I snapped her bra free and sent it flying, I lost every thought. "God, you're beautiful." That was all I could say before I sucked the peak of one breast into my mouth and tongued her nipple to a tight bud.

She groaned and arched against me, so I took her other nipple between my thumb and forefinger and rolled it until it beaded. These breasts were going to star in every fantasy I'd have for the rest of my life. I wanted to kiss them, to suck them, to caress and hold them. I wanted to push them together and slide my cock between them.

Instead, I slid down her body, kissing my way past her soft belly until I held the straps of her thong in my hands.

"Take it off," she ordered, arching her hips to help.

"Hell yes." I did as the woman bid, sliding the scrap of pink down her incredible thighs and pulling them off.

I let go of the fantasy I'd had of her in my head because the reality was so much better. "Perfect," I murmured because I couldn't think of another word. Her eyes were glazed with need, lips swollen from my kiss, nipples flushed from my mouth, thighs shifting with pure want.

"You're perfect," she praised, lifting a finger to my abs.

"Later," I begged as I sank between her thighs, then pushed them wide to reveal her pussy. She was hairless except for a small strip. Just glistening, pink, plump flesh waiting to be pleasured.

My cock throbbed in time with my heartbeat.

I parted her with my fingers and put my mouth to her clit. She cried out, rocking against my lips as her hands gripped my head. The mix of sweet and salt on my tongue sent me reeling. I couldn't get enough of her. My tongue swept from her opening to her clit, then worked at her with soft licks and ravenous growls as she thrashed above me.

But it still wasn't enough.

I stabbed my tongue inside her, and she screamed, her muscles clamping down. Fuck, she was going to be so damned tight when I finally pushed inside her. I fucked her with my tongue as I rubbed my fingers over her clit, keeping her on the edge, but not giving her enough to send her over.

"Connell!" she demanded, tugging at my hair. "What are you doing to me?"

Instead of answering her, I replaced my tongue with my fingers and then sucked her clit. She arched beneath me, rocking, riding my mouth and fingers as I took her higher. Her movements grew jerky as her breaths came even choppier. Then she tensed, and I pressed hard on her clit with my tongue.

This time my name wasn't a demand, but a cry as she came, flooding my fingers with her arousal. So wet. So very wet.

I licked her down, and only when she relaxed completely, I reached for a foil packet from the box in my nightstand.

"Let me." She opened the packet with her teeth, then rolled the condom over my cock in one sure motion. "So cliché, but could you be any bigger?"

"You'll like how big I am in about thirty seconds," I promised her as I laid her back.

"I'm counting on it," she answered with a grin, sweeping her thumb over my lower lip. "Your mouth should be outlawed. That was...incredible."

"Just wait." I lowered my mouth to kiss her and kept kissing her as her hands ran down my back to cup my ass.

"Fuck me, Connell," she whispered in my ear, lifting her knees so I settled at her entrance.

Speechless. She'd rendered me speechless.

I gripped her hip with one hand and buried the other in her curls. Then I pushed inside her with slow-rolling thrusts, keeping my eyes on hers the entire time.

Fuck me, she was so hot. So tight. I locked my jaw and concentrated on her as I thrust in fully. "Holy shit," I groaned against her lips. "Ye feel like a silk vise around me."

"How can you speak?" she groaned and swirled her hips.

"Fuck. Lass. Annabelle. Give me a second here." This would be over in exactly two seconds if she did that again.

"I can't help it," she said with a breathy moan. "You feel so good inside me."

I withdrew and slid back inside. How was it even better?

"Tell me if I'm too rough," I ordered as I rolled into her again and again.

"I can take it. I can take *you*." She planted her feet and arched up for each thrust. "So don't hold back. Take me however you need."

Her teeth nipped at my earlobe, and my control snapped.

Harder. Deeper. I took her with abandon, losing myself in the feel of her, the taste of her, the sounds she made each time I bottomed out inside her. When she ordered me to move faster, I grinned and stayed exactly at the same rhythm as I stroked her higher and further into bliss.

I was going to live here, right between her thighs. Nothing outside this room—this bed—mattered. Just her. Just this. Just us.

Her cries grew louder, and I felt that tension take over, locking her thighs as her orgasm started. "That's it," I praised as I abandoned her hip to slide my thumb between our bodies. I strummed her swollen clit as I fucked her with long, hard, deep strokes, pushing myself past the limits I thought I had.

But that pleasure spiraling down my spine to gather in my balls wasn't waiting any longer, and her loud cries were only spurring me on. "Damn. Annabelle. Ye feel so fucking good, love. You're killing me. Come with me, love."

"Connell," she whispered over and over. When her pitch changed, I pressed on her clit, and she came around me, squeezing me so tight that I stopped fighting my orgasm and gave my body over to it.

My thrusts became as erratic as my breathing, and then it hit. Blinding, star-seeing pleasure burst through me as I slammed as deep as I could go in her welcoming body and emptied myself into her.

I didn't know if had been minutes or hours when I found the strength to raise my head from her neck and kiss her lips. "Are you okay?" I asked, lifting my weight on my elbows to keep from crushing her.

"Uh. huh. Better than okay." She smiled sleepily up at me and traced my face with her fingers. "You're beautiful and very, *very* good at that."

I grinned and kissed her again. I'd been right the first time I'd kissed her. She'd ruined me for anyone else. She was it. The epitome. The standard. Everything. "Give me a minute, and then I'll show ye how good I am at it again."

Her brown eyes sparkled as she licked her lips. "Good, because I wasn't lying. I really do have this shower fantasy."

"Your wish is my command." Whatever fantasy she had, I'd fulfill it. I'd be it.

She might not know it yet, but she was mine, and I'd do whatever was necessary to keep her.

8

ANNABELLE

"*D*inner at Luigi's, ice cream at your favorite spot, and now this?" Connell asked as he drove through the entrance to Sweet Water's drive-in theater. "You must *really* want to spoil me."

I smiled at him. "Just a little," I said. "And I wanted you to see why Sweet Water means so much to me."

Connell navigated the gravel pathways and rows of cars until he found a nice little secluded spot in the back corner near the tree line that bordered the outdoor theater. The clear night sky above twinkled with little pinpricks of light as we hopped out of the truck he'd borrowed for the occasion, rounding it to the bed.

Connell grabbed the thick bundle of blankets I'd packed, and I tucked my picnic basket under my arm as he lined the bed of the truck with quilts and pillows.

"All set," he said, towering above me as he stood in the truck bed. He reached a hand down for me, and I passed him the basket. He chuckled but took it and settled it in the back corner before coming back for me. "Come here," he said, hand outstretched.

I slipped my fingers in his, hiking my foot on the tailgate, but Connell easily hefted me into the truck, not a sign of struggle on his face.

"I've never done this before," he said as we leaned against the pillows. The old theater screen took up the entirety of our viewpoint, an ancient cartoon concession preview dancing across it, illuminating the rows and rows of cars ahead of us. Some people had brought fold-out chairs and sat in front of their cars while others elected for the beds of trucks like Connell and myself. Laughter echoed from the aisle leading to the concession stand at the back of the lot, and I found myself smiling.

"Everyone should experience a drive-in at least once," I said, flipping open the basket and fishing out two small plastic cups. I raised one to him, and he plucked it out of my hand. I retrieved the flask I'd packed, and poured him a knuckle's length of scotch, then did the same in my glass. "Cheers," I said, tapping the rim of his cup with mine before we both took a sip.

His eyebrows raised. "This is my favorite," he said, and heat blazed straight down the center of me at the sight of his tongue swiping the lone drop of scotch off his bottom lip.

"Echo told me," I said. "I wanted to make tonight special for you. As a thank you—"

"How many times do I have to tell ye? You don't need to thank me."

"I know," I said. "But I *do*. You've done so much for Sweet Water." I smirked, tucking my cup into the opened basket before shifting fully to face him. "I guess you running into that statue could be the best thing that ever happened to our town." I nudged him. "Lucky for me."

He laughed softly, nuzzling the soft part of my neck before pulling back to look me in the eye. "Never thought I'd see the day," he said.

"What?" I tilted my head.

"When you thanked me for wrecking your beloved statue," he said. "You were so angry that day in court."

A flush bloomed under my cheeks. "Well, you know how important this community is to me."

"Aye."

"And...and...I may have been rash. I thought you were reckless. I thought you didn't *care* about anything but attention and a laugh."

A muscle in his jaw ticked. "Och."

"I'm sorry," I said. "I know I was wrong."

He shrugged. "Not entirely," he said. "I do love making people laugh."

I swallowed hard, my heart aching in my chest remembering the story of how he'd started making his mother laugh after his father had left them in the cold.

"I already told you about my mother, about what my dad leaving did to her." He raked his hand through his hair. "And in school, with the jokes, I realized one crucial thing."

"What?" I asked, my voice cracking from the truth he laid bare.

He turned to me, his blue eyes open, vulnerable. "If *you're* the one making people laugh, *you're* the one keeping people on their toes from pranks and stunts...they don't look deeper. Don't push for your backstory, and back then, my dad leaving my mother and myself, breaking her the way he did; it was the *last* thing I wanted to share with people."

"And now?"

"I still don't advertise my upbringing," he said.

"But you shared with me."

"You asked," he said. "And I'll never lie to you, Annabelle. Ever."

My head spun at the primal promise in those words, and I didn't have the proper ones to respond. To tell him how much that meant to me. So, instead, I used my lips in another way.

I crushed them against his, so hard and fast he dropped his empty cup as he caught me against him. His hands folded around my back as I rolled half on top of him, my mouth exploring his in a fevered hunger. He tasted like scotch and heat and pure Connell, his scent filling my lungs and making my head spin.

I tangled my fingers in his hair, flicking my tongue against the roof of his mouth. His hand slid lower until he'd found the back of my knee and hitched my leg over his hip, shifting us until we were on our sides, never once breaking the kiss that set my entire being on fire.

"Annabelle," he sighed between my lips, and I trembled from the word, from the pressure of his incredibly hard cock I could feel through his jeans as I shamelessly rocked against it. I knew exactly what he felt like inside me, and I was certain no amount of time or distance could ever make me stop wanting him.

Connell smirked against my lips, clearly pleased with my greediness. He cradled my head with one hand, his other smoothing over my breasts and lower until he'd reached the hem of my skirt. He broke our kiss long enough to gauge my reaction as he slowly, agonizingly slipped his fingers between my thighs.

I nodded, arching slightly against his touch, burning with the need to feel him on me.

He teased me over my lace panties, the rough fabric contrasting deliciously with his gentle caresses.

"Mmm," he moaned against my lips. "You're drenched, love," he said before sucking my tongue into his mouth, causing my breath to catch as chills raced across my skin.

I wiggled until my hand found his hard length, and watched his eyes flare as I popped the button on his jeans and slipped in. He was hot and strong and huge in my hand as I explored him from his head and down, pumping in time to his torturous teases between my thighs.

"Connell," I gasped, my focus splintering as he shoved the lace aside and met my wetness with his fingers.

"Fuck," he said, his lips exploring my neck. "You're brilliant." He slid his fingers right down the center of me, and everything in my body, my being, honed in on that sensation. On the need coursing through my veins. On the fire sizzling just under my skin.

I pumped him in my hand, our eyes locking as he pulled back enough to see my face. He didn't blink, barely *breathed* as he slid one finger inside, then another, until all I could feel or think was *him.*

"You're brilliant," he said again, moving inside me. "Gorgeous," he said, emphasizing his words by going deeper, only to pull his fingers out and slid them in again. I coiled and clenched as I rode his hand, as I lost all sense of time and setting and logic. As I became nothing but pure sensation, a puppet moving to the will of his hands, and sweet *mercy* the man knew how to pluck my strings.

"There she is," he said, grinning that purely male confident smile as he watched me on the brink of explosion. "All you need is a little...*push.*" He pressed his thumb down on that small, aching bundle of nerves and covered my mouth with his own at the same time, swallowing my cry of release. Drinking it in, savoring it as I shattered completely for him.

Slowly, gently, he worked me through the throes of the orgasm, planting me with soft kisses on my lips, my neck, my collarbone, as I could do nothing but lay limp in his arms, trembling from the intensity of it.

My head spun with the buzz from his touch, from the power he held over my body, my heart, and I was certain nothing could ever—

Laughter.

Loud and crystal clear sounded from our right, and I jolted in his embrace.

Drive-in theater.

I'd completely forgotten where we were.

Who I was meant to be.

I quickly scanned the area, sighing slightly when I realized the group of theater-goers were laughing at their own conversation as they returned to their cars, not noticing us at all.

"Omigod," I said, scooching up to a sitting position, covering my face with my hands. "I can't believe I just...we just..."

Connell laughed softly, raising up to sit next to me. "It's all right, love," he said, gently tugging my hands away from my face.

The movie was well into its plot on the screen, the parking lot quiet save for the occasional giggle or the crickets chirping from the trees next to us.

"No, you don't get it," I said, flustered. "I've *never* done that. Not in public. Connell, if someone would've caught us—"

"I wouldn't have let that happen," he said.

"How would you have known?"

"I was fully aware of what was going on around us. If I'd heard someone, I would've stopped us."

A cold bucket of ice-water crashed over my head.

"You were *aware*..." my voice cracked.

Of course, he was. Why wouldn't he be? He wasn't as consumed by me as I was by him.

Damn it.

I was getting in too deep. Losing myself to a man who couldn't possibly feel the same.

"Right." I cleared my throat and straightened my skirts,

my chest fracturing slightly as I did.

"What the hell just happened?" he asked, his brow furrowed.

"Nothing."

"Nah," he said, turning me so that his face filled my vision. "Don't do that. Talk to me."

I sighed.

Fine.

I was a grown woman, after all, I could at least be honest. "It's nothing, honestly, Connell. It makes perfect sense."

His eyes flared. "*What* does?"

"That you wouldn't be as...lost in the moment as I was."

That muscle in his jaw ticked, and he cocked an eyebrow at me. Gently, he tugged my hand in his until he placed it against his still, very hard cock. "Does that feel like I'm not as *into* it as you, Annabelle?"

I gasped, instantly liquid at the firm pressure against my hand, and cursed myself for wanting him so badly. For wanting him to pack us up and take us home where I could ravish him properly.

I tugged my hand back before I could suggest such a thing. "I'm sorry about that," I said, a pang of guilt hitting me. "I didn't mean to get you worked up only to not fin—"

"I don't give a shite about that," he said. "I wanted to please *you*. Don't you get that by now?"

I swallowed hard. "No," I admitted. "I don't get it, Connell. I *so* don't get it." I shook my head, smoothing my fingers through my wild hair. "We can laugh together and be friends and even have fun between the sheets, but we both know I'm not what you really want."

His lips parted, his blue eyes churning with liquid fire. "You're out of your fucking mind."

I gaped at him. "Excuse me?" I whisper-hissed to keep from snapping.

"You are," he said. "If you think that you're not exactly what I want."

"Oh, come on, Connell," I said, arching a brow at him. "We both know I'm nothing more than a convenient fling until the season really starts, and all the perfect bunnies arrive." I smacked my hand on my knee. "Hell, you just admitted you were completely aware of our surroundings while I was on another fucking planet. That's not balanced—"

He took an obvious deep breath, laying his hand over mine. "Annabelle, the only reason, and I'm fucking serious, the *only* reason I knew what was going on around us is because I made an effort to. And it's not fucking easy, but I *know* you. I know how important your professional appearance is to you, and I would never put you in a situation where you'd find yourself vulnerable or open to judgment."

Tears welled behind my eyes.

"If I hadn't made that effort? I wouldn't have stopped at one orgasm. I would've peeled those frilly little panties down your legs, and I would've slid into you right here until ye came so many times I'd have to carry you home. Do you understand me?"

My heart raced, a battle of lust and want and hope swirling until my head spun.

"No one can compare to you," he continued. "And believe me, you are the furthest thing from *convenient*." He laughed a dark laugh. "You're stubborn, argumentative, and a right pain in the arse half the time."

I bit back a grin.

"And I love it. Every. Single. Second. Of. It."

I sucked in a sharp breath as his hand smoothed over my face to cup my cheek.

"I don't care about bunnies." His other hand disappeared behind his back until he'd come back with his phone. He held the cell out at an arm's length until our faces filled the frame. He pressed a tender kiss to my forehead and snapped the picture. "I'll post this right now, showing everyone who exactly I'm with and who I *want*."

I shook my head. "Don't," I said, my voice a ragged whisper.

He sighed. "You don't want people to know we're together."

"Are we?"

He put his phone away. "There is no one else, Annabelle. There hasn't been long since before I hit your beloved statue. And there won't be. Not as long as you'll have me."

My lips parted, two tears rolling down my cheeks. "I'm not what you need—"

"Stop," he said, wiping the tears away with his thumbs. "As long as you'll have me," he said again. "You understand?"

I didn't.

Not really.

I couldn't deny the white-hot chemistry between us. Couldn't deny how we laughed and had fun together. Couldn't deny his tenacity and dedication when it came to learning who I was inside. Couldn't deny how he was the first person I wanted to see in the morning and the last person I wanted to talk to at night. That he'd become my first call when *anything* of interest happened.

And yet...I wasn't his usual type. I had curves, lots of them, and I sure as hell wasn't Instagram-ready like Blaire. If the public saw us together...they'd ridicule him. And that's the last thing I wanted.

But I wanted him *more*.

And for now, that was enough.

I finally nodded, pressing my lips together in what I hoped he could tell was an apology for the outburst.

He sighed, relief churning in his eyes as he tucked me into his side and settled us back against the pillows.

"Now, what the bleeding hell is happening in this film?" he whispered, and a laugh burst from my lips. The icky, heavy tension completely cleared.

And a jolt of ice-cold fear pulsed in my heart as I reeled in that laugh.

Because I realized just how powerful Connell had become in my heart—fully capable of either crushing it, or healing it.

And I was scared to death of which one would win in the end.

9

CONNELL

"Och, and what about that one?" I nodded toward the rookie, who flew by, trying his hardest to catch Cannon. Trying was the correct word. There wasn't a faster skater in the NHL than Cannon Price.

"Maxfield," Logan answered as we leaned over the wall from the bench. "Rookie out of Boston."

"And that one?" I motioned toward the guy in goal next to Sawyer.

"Jansen Sterling." Logan shook his head. "Didn't you at least read all the trading news?"

"Nah. Figured I'd get all the news here anyway." I shrugged and watched as the local skaters took the ice.

It was mid-August, and we had a couple of weeks until our official practices began, but we liked to get together for informal pick-up games as we all got back into town, or in the case of both Logan and I—never leave town.

Cannon flew by and stopped suddenly at the end of the bench, throwing snow.

"I don't know, Price. I think you may be a wee bit out of shape," I jested.

"Fuck off," he muttered as the new kid caught up.

The kid ripped off his helmet and shook out his sweat-laden hair with awe on his face. "How the hell do you move like that?"

Cannon took off his helmet and simply turned away from the kid, dismissing him completely as he climbed in next to us.

"Gossiping like the little school girls you are?" he asked.

"Always," Logan replied with a smirk.

The kid's eyes flew wide as Axel stepped in with us, Lukas Vestergaard at his side.

"Stop scaring the rookies, Cannon," Axel warned.

A corner of Cannon's mouth lifted, but it would have been wrong to call it a smile.

"Go skate, Maxfield. We'll be out once we're done gossiping like the little school girls we are." Axel shooed off the new skater.

"How many newbies are we stuck with?" Lukas asked.

"Five," a voice behind us answered.

We turned to see Asher Silas, the owner of the Reapers, standing with Coach McPherson.

"We took the best they had and even found a goalie for McCoy to train up." Silas nodded toward the goal. "So don't run off the rookies, okay?"

We all muttered our assent as a hulking figure skated our way. He ripped off his helmet as he stood in front of us and glared.

Interesting.

"Who the fuck decided that I have to show up to some bullshit charity gala?" he growled.

"Well, if I knew who the fuck you were, maybe I could answer you," Silas replied, chill as the ice.

"I'm Brogan Grant, your new left wing." Guy lifted his chin a good inch in the air. "Who the fuck are you?"

Every single player in the bench stood still as death.

"I'm Asher Silas, the owner of the Reapers, that's who the fuck I am. Also, you'll be showing up to that *bullshit* charity auction because the contract you signed agreed to any charitable appearances that I deem appropriate on behalf of the Reaper Charitable Foundation. If you have a problem with that, I'm happy to negotiate a contract that removes you from the Reapers." Silas didn't even wait for the guy to respond, he just turned to Coach. "I think I've seen all I need to." He took off down the access tunnel.

"You're the one out LA, right?" Coach asked as if he didn't know. Of course he knew since he was the one who went after the trades.

"Yeah. They call me Demon."

Had to hand it to the arse, he didn't back down.

"They'll be calling you from the minors if you ever mouth off on my ice like that again. Don't test me. I don't let assholes skate on my team." Coach shook his head and headed off to where Langley was flagging him down at the edge of the rink.

Grant watched, then made a sound of appreciation as Langley turned away.

"Look at her again, and I'll remove your balls as a favor because there's no chance in hell you could handle my wife. I don't care what the fuck they call you." Axel walked over the wall—he was that bloody tall—and skated off without another word.

Lukas whistled at Grant and did the same.

"Well, Grant, way to make a first impression," I said with a nod. "Och, and just a heads up, the role of broody bastard has already been taken by Cannon, so you might need to find a new schtick."

"He's not wrong," Logan agreed, slapping Cannon on the back.

Cannon didn't bat an eye at the guy as Grant tried to stare him down. Then he fucking grinned.

Grant swore and skated off.

"What a first-class prick," Logan muttered.

"We should warn Sephie and have her cut him from the gala. No one needs that around a fundraiser," I mused.

"Who the fuck is Sephie?" Cannon snapped and gave me his full attention.

"Persephone? You know, the little blonde who runs the charitable—"

"I know who Persephone is," he barked. "What I don't know is why the fuck you're calling her *Sephie.*"

I blinked, feeling like I'd missed a road sign somewhere. "Uh, because that's her nickname? You can't honestly think a lass that little is going to carry her full name around like that."

"And how the hell do you know it?" He stepped toward me.

"Because I was in her office signing some sticks—hockey sticks, Cannon. You've gone daft, man. Anyway, her dad popped in and called her Sephie." I didn't back up, but it was only because I knew him well enough to know he wasn't going to murder me like the look in his eyes suggested.

He studied me for a long minute and then nodded. Then he climbed over the wall and headed out to the ice.

"What in the bleeding hell was that about?" I asked Logan.

He shook his head, watching Cannon skate off. "No clue."

"Ward! MacDhuibh! Let's go!" Axel called out, forming lines for a scrimmage.

"Shall we kick some newbie arse?" I asked Logan.

"Hell yes."

"So THIS IS IT, huh? The start of the season?" Annabelle tightened the sash around her robe, looked out over the crowded backyard, and sighed. Her sun hat was huge but sexy as hell, and she was wearing the same oversized glasses she'd worn the first day we met.

"You don't have to look like it's the end of the world, lass. It's just our kickoff party." Every Reaper was in the yard was in various states of undress. Some were still fully clothed, and others were already in swimsuits, enjoying the pool.

One of the poor rookies was enjoying the pool fully clothed thanks to ogling Faith, Lukas's wife.

"I know. It just feels like summer is over."

I took her face in my hands and kissed her, taking my time despite the party going on twenty feet away. Nothing ever seemed to matter while I was kissing Annabelle. She parted her lips, and I sank into her, swirling my tongue around hers until she gripped my bare shoulders and moaned.

"Fuck the party, let's go upstairs," I murmured against her lips.

She grinned and shook her head. "It's your party, Connell. We can't just disappear."

"Sure we can." I tugged her against me and filled my hands with her sweet arse. "No one will even know we're gone."

Her hands slipped down my chest, then traced the lines of my abs. "As much as I would love to take you upstairs, there's no chance that's going to happen while you have all these people here."

"I'll kick them out," I offered.

She laughed, and I groaned as she pulled away from me. "Let's go join your guests."

I groaned but took her hand.

"You sure?" she asked, looking down at our entwined fingers.

"I couldn't care less who knows about us. If you're worried about being *public*, then don't stress. No one here will run off to the press." I stood at the giant glass doors and waited for her to make her choice.

"Okay," she said with a nod.

My smile was Cheshire-cat big as we walked onto the patio, then down the steps that led to the pool area.

"I can't believe you bought a splash pad just for the Reaper kids." She shook her head as we passed a few players. The deck was crowded, but there were still a few lounge chairs open over by Echo, where I knew Annabelle would feel most comfortable.

"Well, I figured my kids would like it, too."

She halted.

"Annabelle?" When she dropped my hand, I turned to face her.

"You have kids?" she hissed.

I took off her sunglasses so I could see her eyes and noticed they were almost as big as the lenses had been.

"No, lass. I don't have children. At least not yet. But maybe one day."

She blinked away the shock and blushed. "Oh. Okay. Sorry, I just realized that there is so much I don't know about you."

"There's time." All the time she wanted. I wasn't going anywhere.

"So, you want kids?" she asked, taking my hand again.

I watched some of the younger generations of Reapers play in the splash pad and nodded. "Aye. I'd like a family."

"Annabelle!" Echo called out and waved us over.

"Hey!" Annabelle dropped her bag on the empty chair closest to Echo's.

"I'm going to get in," I whispered in her ear.

"I think I'm just going to visit here with Echo." She clutched the corners of her robe together.

I kissed her forehead, and when I pulled away, Echo was open-mouthed staring at us. "I think you're the sexiest woman on the planet, and if you bring that incredible arse into the pool, I'll make it worth your while," I growled in her ear.

She rolled her eyes at me and gave me a little shove.

"Take care of her," I ordered Echo.

"Uhhh, that's my line," she said with a huff, her gaze flickering between Annabelle and me.

I gave her a mock salute and headed for the water. A water gun fight, two slides, and two more rookies dunked, I looked over from the pool and nearly swallowed my tongue.

Annabelle walked toward me in a two-piece, pulling her hair up as she moved.

It was bright pink, with boyshort bottoms and a halter top that did unholy things with her breasts—or rather, it made *me* want to do unholy things with them.

She gave me a sinful smile and climbed down the ladder into the middle of the pool.

"Fuck, lass," I said quietly so the kids wouldn't hear me. "Ye look incredible."

She wound her arms around my neck and kissed my lips. "Where's the *worth-my-while*?"

I kissed her long and harder than was decent for the current crowd as I backed her against the edge of the pool. "If there weren't minors around, your *worth-your-while* would be inside you right now."

"MacDhuibh, get over here!" Logan ordered from the volleyball net we had strung near the end of the pool. "We need you!"

I sighed, noting that his girlfriend had the camera out. Jesus, that woman was always posting shit.

"You heard what they said," Annabelle giggled. "They need you."

"Well, I need ye."

"Go win your game, and we'll see about it."

"Fine," I pouted but kissed her again. "Besides, one more moment over here, and the rest of the pool would see your *worth-your-while*."

She laughed and shoved me toward the guys. It was the sweetest sound I'd ever heard, and I found myself echoing it. Who would have thought a few months ago that the proper little lass with the rule book would be the sinful ass I'd be obsessed with?

For the first time in my life, I felt a sense of balance, and it was just as comforting as it was terrifying because I knew in this situation, she held all the power.

ANNABELLE

"*Y*ou certainly know how to throw a party," I said, sliding the last bit of Tupperware into Connell's fridge. The last stragglers from the night had just gone home, and it was well past eleven.

"Aye," Connell said as I rounded the corner to meet him in the living room, and I stopped suddenly at the sight of him.

The man laid back on his hunter green, tufted, armless chaise. Shirtless, a pair of black Reaper athletic pants hugging his hips, showing off those damned impossible v-lines he had. His eyes were half-closed, his hair damp from the shower he'd just taken, feet bare.

"Sweet mercy," I said before I could stop myself, and his eyes widened a bit.

"You know what that southern accent does to me?" He smiled.

"Says the Scottish man who looks like that simply *sitting*." I motioned to the perfection of his body, half-heartedly shaking my head.

He cocked an eyebrow at me. "You're one to talk, love," he

said, his accent burring those r's and skittering over my skin. "Walking around in that bikini earlier? I thought I might die from wanting you."

Heat flared down the middle of me, at the desire in his eyes, the primal need in his tone.

I'd never felt more desirable or beautiful in my entire life.

This...*this* is what it felt like to be wanted on every possible level.

The realization of that absolute truth filled every crevice of my body with an aching hunger I couldn't possibly survive.

I shaped my lips in what I hoped was close to Connell's usual mischievous grin, and delight rippled through me as his eyes tracked my every move toward him. He reached for me when my knees hit the side of his chaise, but I tsked him.

He cocked a brow, the pulse spiking at his neck as I guided his arms up and above him, securing them on the lip of the chaise.

"Stay," I demanded, then took my time exploring his skin with the pads of my fingers, then followed the trail with my lips, pausing to appreciate the ink decorating his muscled right bicep. I traced the whorls of ink with my tongue, then kissed my way up the light stubble on his jaw, and then moved lower. Over his hard chest and the ridges of his abdomen until I reached the bulge not at all hiding beneath his pants.

I raked my teeth over the fabric, wicked surprise fluttering through me when I realized he wore nothing beneath. I glanced up at him while I teased him with feather-light strokes. He kept his hands where I'd secured them, but his muscles flexed with the effort, and his hips jerked with each teasing touch I issued.

Hooking my fingers into the waistband, I slowly tugged them down and tossed them to the side, his considerable length springing free. My mouth watered, and my head spun with the consuming desire I had for this man. With the power coursing through my veins, I took a few steps back, peeling off my clothes so he could see every inch of me. I didn't bother reaching for the light switch, didn't even feel the impulse to. That alone would've been enough to tell me how much Connell meant to me, but the need pulsing in time with my heart confirmed it.

Fire licked my skin as his eyes trailed the length of my body and back to my eyes.

I settled one knee between his, the other over one of his thighs as I knelt over him. I fisted his length, hard as granite in my hand, and didn't hesitate to take him in my mouth.

"Fuck," he hissed, arching upward.

I smiled around his cock, using my tongue to swirl around his head, moaning at the taste of him—salt and heat and pure Connell. I sucked and stroked before teasingly trailing my tongue down the side until I'd reached his base and traveled back up again. He writhed beneath me, his biceps flexing from the pressure of keeping his hands where I'd left them.

Sucking his head into my mouth again, I moaned around him as he lifted his knee between my thighs, adding a bit of pressure to my tease of a dance. So carefully, slowly, I took him deeper, as far as I could possibly go, my heart racing with the control, with the sexy as sin hisses coming from Connell's mouth.

Then his hands were in my hair, and his cock sprang from my mouth with a little pop as I shook my head. "Ah, ah," I chided.

He groaned from the sudden change, and I smirked at him, eyeing those hands.

Fire danced in his eyes as he raised them and put them back above his head.

And I might've came right there from the shift in control, from the way he allowed me to take the reins.

But I needed him back in my mouth.

And so I dove back in, reveling in the taste of him, in the way he hardened inside my mouth when I lightly, carefully grazed his hard flesh with my teeth. And just when I could *feel* that shift in him, just when I *knew* I had him, I pulled back.

A growl of protest rumbled from his chest, but I wasted no time in settling myself over him, positioning his slick tip at my drenched entrance.

"Annabelle," he said through clenched teeth. "Condom," he could only manage one-word sentences.

I paused, waiting. "I want to feel you inside me," I said. "I'm on the pill. Is that okay?"

"*Fuck, yes,*" he answered, and I sank onto him in one smooth motion.

I threw my head back, a gasp ripping from my lips at the way he filled *every* inch of me. The way I went tight and loose at the same time. The way I couldn't *think* around him but needed so, so much more.

I rocked my hips, bracing my hands on his firm chest for leverage. Up and down and back and forth, I rode him hard but slow, squeezing out every drop of pleasure I could. Savoring the feel of him, the scent of him, the way his blue eyes blazed as he watched me. Every inch of me coiled like a tight spring. I reached up and grabbed his hands, placing them on my breasts, needing to feel him everywhere.

A sigh of pure relief left his lips at the freedom, and he hauled himself upward until we were chest to chest, lips to lips.

And I stilled atop him as he kissed me with such tenderness, such *care* that I couldn't contain the pleasured cry that escaped my lips.

His hands raked through my hair and tilted my head for a better angle as he kissed me deeper. He took his time to work more moans from my lips, and he drank them down like his favorite scotch.

I wrapped my arms around his neck, not an inch of space separating us as I began to move again. Slowly torturing us both. Each roll of my hips made the pair of us tremble from the exertion, from the rippling electricity sparking in every place we needed, wanted. Until we were breathless and sweat-slicked. Until I was sure I would die from wanting this man, from feeling this fucking good.

"Annabelle," he sighed my name, his voice raspy with desire. "Look at me."

I met his eyes, smiling at the delight in them.

"You're brilliant," he said. "Beautiful. Come with me." The primal tenor in his voice skittered down my spine, undoing every sense of control I may have possessed.

And then he *lifted* as I rocked down on top of him, and release barreled through me, bursting and sparking so hard my eyes saw stars. A gasp tore through me as I threw my head back, gripping his shoulders for support as he hardened infinitely more as he found his own release inside me.

We sat there, my forehead against his, connected in more ways than physical as we caught our breath. Connell gently lifted us from the chair, kissing me sweetly as he carried us upstairs to his room, where he helped me get cleaned up before tucking me into his bed.

"Now what?" I whispered in the quiet dark as he stood by the bed.

He knew what I meant.

Knew my concerns with the upcoming season.

He reached into the drawer of his nightstand, plucking out a small metal object and handing it to me.

"A key?" I asked, palming the thing.

He climbed into bed next to me, his warm, naked body melting me all over again as he settled behind me. He covered us with his comforter, tucking my back against his chest, his chin over my shoulder.

"And I cleared out two drawers for you in my dresser," he said. "I want to spend as much time as possible with you. So, do with that what you will, love," he said, motioning to the key in my hand.

I slipped it under the pillow on what had become *my* side of his bed and turned enough to meet his eyes. "Okay," I said.

"Okay?" He arched a brow at me.

"Let's do this. For real."

A wide, genuine smile shaped his lips before he crushed them against mine.

I finally surrendered this one part of myself to him, the one I'd been holding onto because of the skepticism I had about what would happen when the season truly started. But Connell made those doubts disappear with every sweet, gentle touch of his lips. Had made them disappear as we'd grown closer—in friendship, in lust, in...everything.

I closed my eyes, opening for him again, wider this time. Letting him *in* another inch, dangerously close to all the way down in my *soul*.

And he must've felt the subtle shift because he didn't let me sleep a wink that night.

* * *

"Now *that's* a nice background," Lacy said over my shoulder, and I bit back my smile. She practically skipped back to her desk. "I'm so proud of you."

I rolled my eyes. "It's just a picture," I said.

She arched a brow at me.

"Okay, it's a hot picture," I relented, gazing at my new

115

computer wallpaper. A simple shot of Connell and myself, his arm tucking me in tight. But it was the *way* he gazed down at me that made the picture practically catch fire. The hunger in his eyes, the wicked grin on his lips.

Sweet mercy, this man made me feel like the most beautiful woman in the world.

Like I was the only woman in the world.

Cold, familiar doubt crept past the flames gently whirring in my core, whispering icy facts into the back of my mind.

The real season will start soon.

Away games.

Women in every state want him.

How could any man withstand a constant stream of perfection?

I shook my head in an attempt to clear it and clicked on the documents I *should* be working on, effectively covering the happy picture on my screen.

Work.

Work was my number one passion before Connell plowed into my life on a four-wheeler with a Scottish accent and an irresistible laugh.

I buried myself in work, shoving all other thoughts away until the next thing I knew, Lacy was tapping my shoulder in way of goodbye and clocking out for the evening.

I finished up payroll for the week and then shut everything down, totally, mentally exhausted. After locking the building up, I strolled to my car, thoughts of a glass of wine and a good book dominating my mind, knowing Connell had been swamped with preseason skates. My phone buzzed in my pocket, and I fished it out after I'd settled into the driver's seat.

Connell: Home yet?

I bit back my grin as I texted back.

Me: Just in the car now.

Connell: Good. Go to my place instead.

Me: I thought you would be out late with the boys?

Connell: Aye. Team morale. But I'd love it if I found you in my bed when I came home.

A thrill rushed through me.

Me: Even if I'm asleep?

Connell: Always. What do you say?

Me: I guess you'll just have to wait and find out.

Connell: Tease.

I set my cell in the cup holder and took the road that led me to Reaper Village.

An hour later, I'd slipped into my favorite silk pajama set and sank into Connell's king-sized bed, drowning in the luxury of his soft sheets and thick blankets. Lucky for me, he kept my favorite wine on hand, and after half a glass, I was blissfully relaxed. Totally at home. Enough to fall into an easy sleep where doubts and fears didn't exist.

THE BED SHIFTED BEHIND ME, a sturdy weight rolling my body slightly. I blinked away the haze of sleep, but just barely as I parted my lids.

"Sorry, love," Connell whispered, his lips at my ear as he settled behind me. "Didn't mean to wake you."

Something inside me utterly relaxed as he tucked my back against his chest, his arms encasing me to him. A settled, solid feeling clicked into place as if something had been missing while he was gone. Now that he was home, everything felt put back in its proper spot.

"How was the morale boosting night?" I asked, trying desperately to shake myself awake.

"Hilarious," he whispered, a soft chuckle vibrating from his chest. "One of the rookies made a right *galoot* of himself trying to woo a waitress who was clearly not interested."

"*Galoot?*" I murmured, tilting my head.

"Idiot," he explained, his nose trailing the seam of my neck, eliciting chills across my skin.

"Ah," I said. "How many ways do you have of saying idiot? I need you to buy me a Scottish dictionary or something."

He laughed again. "I think you're still asleep."

"Am not," I said, though I half was. "Like that song," I said, my head sinking heavy against his bicep that he'd slipped under me.

"What song?"

"The one you hummed at the office constantly."

"Ah," he said. "I didn't realize you were paying attention."

"I was," I admitted.

"It's called *Caledonia*," he whispered. "I don't think there's a Scot alive who doesn't know it. It's about a man who's lost his way but is reminded about what truly matters in the world. He thinks about his roots, about what is most important in life." He gently kissed my neck. "I couldn't stop thinking about it after I met you."

"Why?" I sighed, forcing my eyes to open.

"Because I saw you, heard that smart mouth, and I felt *home*."

I swallowed hard, my brow furrowing as I tried to figure out if this was a dream or not. I shifted against him, prepared to roll over and fully wake up, but he held me tight.

"Sleep, Annabelle," he said, kissing my neck again.

I settled against him, sinking further into myself as I interlocked our hands. "I'm glad you're home safe," I said, already slipping back into slumber.

"I'm glad you were here to come home to," he said.

"Me too," I whispered before falling back into the deep sort of sleep that only came from the complete and utter relaxation of security.

. . .

I DIDN'T WAKE Connell the following morning, knowing he had to be wrecked from how late they'd been out last night. But I kissed him softly before leaving for work, my heart lifted from what I hoped had been real and not a dream last night.

The doubts were still there, but his words, his body sheltering mine throughout the night...they helped chase them away. Helped me dare to believe that maybe, just maybe, what we had was real and would withstand the trials his life naturally would throw at us.

11

CONNELL

*T*here were nights when I was on, and nights when I was on *fire*. I knocked the puck loose from Tampa's newest center, and took it down the boards, firing it off to Cannon just past the blue line.

The crowd roared as he flew by their defense and fired it in. The lamp lit, and the noise level in the arena shot to a new decibel.

I pounded Cannon's back as we filed into the bench for the shift change. It was our first home preseason game, and attendance was already at capacity. The thing about winning the Stanley Cup was that people expected you to do it again. And again.

My gaze went to the family box like it had the whole game. Annabelle sat with Faith, a wide smile on her face as she waved. I gave her a nod and put my attention back on the game. Having her here was damned distracting, but I wouldn't trade it for anything. Besides, it was the first game she'd ever seen, so I was sure the novelty would wear off.

Or not. I almost missed a shift change because I had my eye on Annabelle again.

By third period we were up three to one, and Lukas put another one in at the buzzer for the four-one win. Damn, did I love the feel of a win.

We came off the ice and hit the showers. Preseason meant zero press for the majority of us, which included me.

"Good job, Sterling," I told the rookie goalie as I hauled my bag out of the locker room.

"All five minutes that I played?" he asked with a wry grin.

"Did ye let any in during those five minutes?" I asked, half out the door.

"No," he answered, rubbing his hand over his hair.

"Good job, Sterling," I repeated with a grin, then walked out. I'd give the kid some proper hazing over the next few weeks, but not today. Today he deserved the win, just like the rest of us.

Next week gave me ample time to work up a proper prank to welcome him to the team.

I turned down the hallway toward the ice, near the area I'd asked Annabelle to meet me.

"No, seriously, he asked me to wait here."

Annabelle's voice echoed down the concrete hall, and I picked up my pace at the sound of her agitation.

"Right, like he asked *all* of us," another feminine voice countered.

"Look, honey, I've seen his type, and you aren't it, bless your little heart," another woman added.

Bloody hell.

I turned the corner and saw Wade—one of the security guys—ushering a group of women out of the hall, including Annabelle.

"Wade, hold on a minute," I called out.

He paused and lowered his outstretched arms when he saw me. "Sorry, Mr. MacDhuibh. I don't know how they snuck in here."

"I didn't sneak," Annabelle argued with narrowed eyes, crossing her arms over her chest. "I'm with *him*." Shit, her face was bright red.

The lass was pissed and likely embarrassed, which was even worse.

One of the bunnies behind her scoffed. "Yeah, right. And I'm with Sawyer McCoy."

"Wade, kick those three out," I motioned toward the women with the skin-tight jeans and cropped hockey jerseys. "The classy one is with me, aren't you gorgeous?"

Annabelle cocked an eyebrow at me but uncrossed her arms from her black, form-fitted Reaper jacket.

"Come on, Annabelle, let's go home, lass." I held out the hand that wasn't carrying my sticks. For the barest of seconds, I worried that she might turn me down.

"It's a good thing you're hot, MacDhuibh," she said with a tilt of her head, but she took my hand.

I didn't miss the way one of the bunny's jaws dropped, and neither did Annabelle.

"Wade, she's always allowed back here, okay? I can get her a pass or whatever she needs, but she has full access," I told the guard.

"Absolutely, Mr. MacDhuibh. I'll make sure the other guys know, but it would help if Mrs. Pierce-Nyström got her a badge. Ma'am, I'm sorry. But it's my job to keep...fans out of this area."

"No offense taken," Annabelle replied softly, but her hand tightened in mine.

Wade ushered the other women out the door as Annabelle and I turned to head toward the parking lot.

"You know, that might not have happened if you were wearing my jersey," I teased. But the thought had merit. Just the idea of her in nothing but my jersey stirred my cock. My name on her back. My number. Mine.

I knew I was in for it when she huffed a fake laugh.

She was silent on the thirty-minute drive home, and by the time we pulled into the garage, I'd played out every possible argument in my head, trying to arm myself with rebuttals for whatever she came up with.

"Does that happen a lot?" she asked as we walked into the house.

"Wade kicking fans out of the halls?" I dropped my keys on the counter.

"Women waiting in the halls," she answered softly, tucking her chin.

"Fuck," I muttered. Of all the arguments I'd run through, this was the one I feared most. "Come with me."

I held out my hand and sent up a prayer of thanks when she took it and followed me upstairs. We didn't stop until we reached the large shower in the master bedroom. Letting go of her hand, I stepped inside and turned on the water, then got out before it could soak me.

"Get naked." I stripped off my shirt.

Her mouth popped open. "I'm sorry?"

"I'll answer the question once you're naked."

She looked at me like I'd lost my mind, but started stripping. Great, and now I was as hard as the tile in the shower. Clearly, I hadn't thought this part out well enough. But how could I not be when she bared every delectable curve?

I almost forgot the whole purpose of doing this up here when she stepped out of her purple lace panties and stood there in all her perfection.

"Shite. God give me strength," I muttered a prayer.

Taking her hand, I pulled her into the massive shower. Then I pressed Annabelle against the water-warmed stone wall and caged her with my palms on either side of her.

"Why are we naked?" she challenged, only letting her gaze dart down my chest before jerking it back to my face.

"I thought it through and decided it's harder to argue while you're naked."

Her jaw dropped, and not in a good way.

"Think about it, lass. Have we ever traded cross words while we were both undressed?" I leaned in just enough so she could feel how badly I wanted her.

She rolled her eyes, but a faint smile lifted her lips.

"Listen to me, Annabelle." My voice dropped. "Yes, there are always women in the hallways at the rink. They're in the hotel bars, and the elevators and the really sneaky ones are outside our hotel rooms. I'll never lie to you, lass."

Her gaze dropped, and I lifted her chin with my thumb.

"But I'll never touch one of them. Not as long as you're mine. Ye have my word." That was something I didn't give lightly. I wondered if she knew that.

"Our lives couldn't be any more different," she whispered as her hands grazed my waist. "And I'm not saying that I don't trust you, but confronting the reality is hard to swallow."

"You'll hear things. It can't be helped. You'll hear rumors that I'm sleeping around at away games. You'll see old pictures of me in the tabloids that they'll publish like they're new. You'll have a million reasons to doubt me, and only one reason trust me." I just hoped it was enough, that my strong, stubborn Annabelle wouldn't take the easy way out and run.

"Which is?" she asked, running her fingers down my back, interrupting the streams of hot water from the showerheads.

"I only want ye. There's no other woman who tempts me like ye do. Who gets me hard with a look or a whisper. I'll never go looking for what I have right here. Nothing else compares. I'll never do anything to jeopardize what we have. You don't have to worry about those women in the halls or the bars. All I see is ye." And seeing her was a major reason that my brilliant idea of having this argument in the shower was turning out to be not so brilliant. Her body was close, and warm, and soft and so fucking distracting.

She swallowed. "That sounds like more than one reason."

"Not really. It's all because when I think about ye, I'm realizing more every day that I'm falling—"

She clamped her hand over my mouth.

"Don't you dare say it. Don't even *think* it." She shook her head. "You start leading me down that road, and it will only break my heart when you finally realize that a summer fling can't hold a candle to the life you really lead."

If not for the panic in her eyes, I'd have said the words anyway. I'd have made her listen to me. But there was a plea in those brown depths that I couldn't ignore. She wasn't ready, and I had to respect that, or what the hell were we really doing? Wasn't that what a relationship was? Supporting your partner?

I licked her palm, and she gasped, snatching her hand away.

"Okay. Then let's get something straight. This, right here with you, is my real life. My home. My town. My Annabelle." I kissed the skin just beneath her jaw to punctuate my sentences.

"Connell," she sighed, letting her head fall back against the wall.

"Now, has your question been answered to your satisfaction?" I asked against her neck.

"I'll—" she gasped as I lowered my mouth to her breast, "—always worry, but I trust you."

My heart stuttered at the sweet honesty of those words. Maybe it wasn't the same declaration that I was ready to make—that I was falling in love with her, but I'd take it.

"Then let me give you another thought to replace the worry," I said with a smirk as our eyes locked. "Every time you see one of those women—" I kissed a path down her belly. "I want you to smile and remember that you're the only woman I get on my knees for."

I did just that, lifting one of her thighs over my shoulder. Then I parted her with my fingers and kissed her clit.

"Connell!" she cried out as one of her hands splayed in my hair.

"Ye taste so bloody good." I licked and sucked at her relentlessly, until her head thrashed against the stone above me and she started rocking against my face, chasing her own pleasure.

I kept her right at the edge, where her breaths came in stuttered little huffs. She was so easy to please. So responsive. I'd never enjoyed giving a woman pleasure this much in my entire life. It was as if hers only drove mine higher.

Her cries pitched higher, and her thighs tensed. I raked my teeth over her clit and then sucked on the swollen little bud. She came with a scream that echoed off the stone walls, bucking against my mouth.

I stood while she was still coming, rolling through the aftershock, letting her thigh slide to my waist. Dipping to accommodate her height, I fit my cock to her slippery entrance and thrust home.

If she wouldn't let me use words to tell her how I felt, I'd show her.

She convulsed around me, her pussy gripping me like a velvet fist. I groaned at the exquisite feel of her, then grabbed her other thigh and lifted her against the wall.

"I can't get enough of ye," I growled right before I kissed her.

My tongue moved in time with my cock, taking her in every way possible with hard, deep strokes. Fuck, the bare feel of her was almost too much. She was liquid fire, her body rippling and squeezing mine as if she'd been designed to push me to the very edge of my sanity.

"Baby," she whispered, gripping my neck as I pounded into her.

The endearment nearly made me come. My eyes crossed momentarily as I struggled against my body's needs. "There's nothing like this in the entire world," I told her as I moved within her.

When she whimpered and swirled her hips, I adjusted my grip on her, leveraging her against the wall so I could change our angle. Then I thrust over and over, each slide rubbing my pelvis over her clit.

"Fuck. Fuck. FUCK!" she yelled as she came again.

This time, she took me over the edge with her, my hips jerking against hers as I came hard, spilling myself inside her sweet body as I yelled her name.

We stood just like that until my knees stopped shaking.

Then I washed her—and me—from head to toe and carried her to bed, where I started all over again. I made love to her softly, slowly, bringing her back to blinding pleasure twice more before we slept.

As she drifted off with her head tucked against my shoulder, I quietly vowed that I'd prove to her that this wasn't the summer fling she thought it was. This was real. I'd had enough flings to know the difference.

This wasn't a summer thing.

This was a forever kind of thing.

I just had to prove it to her.

ANNABELLE

"*A*nnabelle!" Blaire squealed from across the parking lot, her heels clicking against the pavement as she hurried toward where I stood next to Echo.

"Hi, Blaire," I said, awkwardly accepting her friendly hug. "Thanks for coming," I said, eyeing her heels. "Though it may be difficult to do a 5K in pumps?"

"Oh," she waved me off. "I came to cheer for Logan. And take pictures. 5Ks aren't really my thing," she admitted with a shrug.

Echo snorted, not even attempting to hide her eye roll.

I gently nudged her but smiled at Blaire. "Well, thank you for the support."

"Absolutely," she said, her cell already in hand. "I'm going to get some great shots and get this event *tons* of exposure. It's so neat that you handled all this yourself!"

I beamed with pride, scanning the crowd of Sweet Water citizens that had gathered for the fundraiser and celebration for the opening of the ostrich reserve. "I didn't do it totally alone," I said.

Blaire smiled but didn't glance up from her phone. "Oh, I

know," she said, fingers flying over her screen. "The picture Connell posted of the two of you? To. Die. For!" she laughed. "I think I heard the cry of every girl in town."

I swallowed hard, heat rising to my cheeks.

Of course, Connell had asked permission before taking our relationship public, but I couldn't fight off the shock that still rocked me that we were official. Just as I couldn't squash that small part of me that couldn't let go of the doubt, of the very possible reality that I would wake up one day and find myself the butt of some twisted joke where I had believed I lived in a world where a man like Connell could love me.

That's not fair.

No. It sure as hell wasn't. Connell had been nothing but good to me. More than good. He was perfect. But the world had reared me on pain, and it had taken years for me to learn to love myself for who and what I was. And while *I* was there, it was sometimes still hard to believe that someone else might...someone who was used to perfection like Blaire, not city clerks from small-town Sweet Water.

"Babe!" Blaire shouted, waving to Logan, who stood near the ticket table, collecting his number. She hurried off without another glance in our direction.

"Something about that girl," Echo said, her eyes narrowed in Blaire's direction.

"Stop," I said, laughing as I hooked our arms together. "Logan adores her."

She snorted. "Maybe pregnancy has made me more irritable?"

"No way," I said, a bit sarcastically. She pinched my arm but smiled.

"You sure you want to walk this thing with me?" she asked.

"Absolutely," I said. "You remember gym class for me.

What a nightmare." I eyed my chest. "Who could possibly run with *these* giant things?"

Echo laughed. "They are quite glorious."

We chuckled as we stopped at the ticket table where a slew of Reapers huddled in random groups.

All.

Shirtless.

Sweet mercy, it was no wonder even Charleston's press had shown up for the event. There were enough muscles on display to tempt even the most chaste of high society. Each Reaper had elected to wear their paper number plastered over the shorts that hugged their massive thighs.

"Not a bad sight," Echo said, her eyes firmly locked on her fiancé Sawyer. "Not a bad sight at all."

I smiled at her. "And the generosity," I said. "Is the real kicker. They've all donated. I don't know how I'll ever thank them enough."

"I'm sure you've found creative ways to thank *one* Reaper in particular enough," she teased, and I nodded.

"Still," I said. "I'll never be out of his debt."

"Is that how you view it?"

I pressed my lips together, electing not to answer.

"Where is he, anyway?" she asked. "I assumed he'd be the first one here."

I checked my cell again, sighing at the lack of texts. "I'm not sure," I admitted and hated the way my voice cracked. Hated the way the doubt snaked its way into my blood. "Maybe he got tied up."

"*Every* other Reaper is here."

"Right. But maybe—"

Echo's eyes widened, and a huge smile stretched her matte blue lips. "Omigod." She grabbed my shoulders and spun me around.

A laugh ripped from my chest, and I tried to quell the sound by covering my mouth with my fingers.

Connell had arrived.

Dressed in a full-body ostrich costume.

His mischievous smile peeked out from what would be the ostrich's neck, the giant head and beak bobbing above him. His entire body covered, the tight black fabric shaped his legs and arms, but the body of the bird filled out his usual carved middle.

"You didn't," I gasped as he bowed before me, the ostrich head nearly bopping me on the nose.

"Aye, but I did." He stood up straight, hands propped on his hips. "You like?"

I laughed, nodding. "*Love.* But you're going to be so hot."

He stepped closer, towering over me as he slipped a hand around my waist. "Aren't I always?"

I playfully smacked his chest.

"Hi, Echo," he said without breaking our gaze.

"Hi, Connell," she said, a mocking tease in her tone. "Love the outfit."

"I'm committed."

"That's for certain."

He squeezed me closer to him, planting a long, languid kiss on my lips. To my ultimate horror, the crowd *cheered*, Echo included.

Heat blazed on my cheeks, but I couldn't stop my smile as Connell released me. "Don't you have to kick us off, love?"

I blinked the lust from my eyes and nodded, heading toward the ticket booth where a microphone waited. My fingers trembled slightly as I gripped the mic, but I took a steadying breath, focusing on what this day meant for me, for Sweet Water.

"In the 1930s, Sweet Water was put on the map for its high-stakes ostrich races," I said, the crowd quieting at my voice booming through the speakers. "And today, while the races aren't the same, the value of the bird is. To Sweet Water, the ostrich will always be our saving grace, and I'm beyond honored that with some hard work and a little help from valued citizens..." I glanced over at Connell in his ridiculously amazing costume. "The birds are back!"

A round of applause erupted, and only after they quieted did I speak again.

"I'd like to thank you all for coming out to today's momentous event. After the 5K, I'd like to invite you to meet the new ostriches of Sweet Water," I said, motioning to the building behind me that contained the entirety of the ostrich reserve—complete with proper living conditions, food, and rooms for medical needs if necessary.

"And," I said, adding purely off-script. "If you could spare a second today, please find the man in the ostrich costume." I pointed at Connell, smiling. "Without his generosity—and the entirety of the Carolina Reapers—none of this would be possible. So please seek him out, and thank him and the Reapers for their generous support of our community additions."

I'd never seen Connell look humble or embarrassed, but I daresay he wore a combination of the two as he grinned back at me.

"Now, without further ado," I said. "Let's get this party started!"

I set the mic back on the table, ushering to the back of the line that had formed behind the starting mark. Then I nodded to Lacy, who stood on the stairs poised above the race. She nodded back and fired the pop-gun, the loud boom kicking off the race.

A mass of shirtless Reapers took off, followed by a slower trail of citizens who were not professional athletes. Connell hung back for a moment, bouncing on the balls of his feet.

He planted a kiss on my lips again before taking off in the costume.

"If you die of heatstroke I'll be very put out!" I yelled, and he spun around, innocently raising his arms before spinning back around and sprinting to catch up with his boys.

I met up with Echo, and we adapted a slow pace at the back of the line.

"I've never seen you this happy," she said. "And I witnessed you get an autograph from JT after an NSYNC concert."

I chuckled, remembering the moment from our childhood. "I *am* happy. Look at this place." I motioned to the building we passed.

"Look at it indeed," my father's voice echoed from behind us, and we paused.

"You made it!" I said, throwing my arms around his neck. "I didn't think you could?"

He hugged me back, then started walking with Echo and myself. "I couldn't miss this," he said. "I'm so proud of you," he said.

"Thanks, Daddy." Pride welled in my chest as we walked.

"And the man in the costume?"

"Connell," I said. "You remember him from—"

"The barbecue," daddy cut me off. "How could I forget?"

Echo snorted from my right, and Dad laughed from my left, no doubt remembering my insistence we were just friends. My how things had changed.

Dad's eyes found Connell in his costume, eons ahead of us, dead center in a pack of shirtless Reapers. "I like him."

I gaped at him, shock barreling through me. I don't know if I'd ever heard him say those words in my life about a boy I liked.

"Me too," Echo agreed.

"He's good for you," Daddy continued, folding his hands behind his back in that reserved way he had.

"What makes you so sure?"

"Look at you," he said, then pointed behind us to the building. "Look at that. He's pushed you, supported you, and had you laughing along the way."

I couldn't argue with him on that.

"I want him to come over for dinner soon," he said.

"Oh, Daddy, I don't know…" I bit my lip.

"Are you not together?" he challenged.

"We are, but…"

"But what?"

I huffed. "I don't know where it's going, okay? I don't know how serious it is."

"It seems quite serious."

"Just because he posted a picture doesn't mean—"

"I'm talking about the way he looks at you, Annabelle, not a damn social media post. Which you know I have no patience for."

I sighed, and Echo snorted again but remained silent.

"Darling," he said, stopping our pace to grip my shoulders. "I only meant that I approve of him, and I'd like to get to know him better in a setting that doesn't include the entire Clarke clan. When *you're* ready. Deal?"

I nodded, hugging him again.

"Would it be so bad?" he whispered.

I tilted my head as he released me.

"To finally let go and let yourself be loved in the way you deserve?"

Echo cleared her throat, spinning on her heels in a desperate attempt not to acknowledge the truth bomb my father had just laid bare between us. But that was my father, no bullshit. He always had been able to see through me so much more than my mother, who had doted on Savannah.

134

"I'm trying," I admitted. "I promise."

"Good," he said, smiling at me. "Now, I believe I'll rally with the press and tell them how incredible my daughter is and how her work will put Sweet Water on the map again."

I smiled at him, waving as he walked in the opposite direction, back toward the crowd still gathered around the building.

"Well," Echo said as we resumed our pace. "Daddy Clarke still doesn't pull any punches."

I laughed. "Never has."

"He's right, though," she said. "You know that. Don't you?"

I eyed up the race, where I could barely make out the Reaper boys and my ostrich man in the midst of them. "Yes," I said. "I know."

"But?" Echo pushed.

"But normal schedules are about to take over," I said. "The real test has yet to come."

"Not everyone is like Atlanta," she said, referring to my ex. She'd long since called him by his name. "And you know I *do* have some insight on loving a man with that same schedule."

"I know," I said. "But, it's different."

"How?"

I chewed on my lip, contemplating. "You couldn't care less what the public thinks of you."

She pursed her lips.

"In the best way," I added. "And you look amazing next to Sawyer."

She glared at me. "And you look amazing next to Connell."

I nodded. "I know. I do. I feel it. But...the public. Will they accept it? I'm not exactly the type you see plastered over their media pages."

"Who gives a flying fuck if they accept it or not?"

"Exactly," I said, snapping my fingers. "*Who* indeed."

"I'm not following."

"What if it's Connell? In the end, what if it's *him* who can't handle it? Can't take the scrutiny of our relationship under a microscope. Of them analyzing my looks and comparing them to every other damn model-worthy bunny out there?"

"That's completely unfair to him, for one," she said. "And for two, you *love* who you are. You're gorgeous. You've never let any of this bother you before."

"I've never dealt with this level of exposure before, Echo. This is *nationwide*. Not contained within the small town of Sweet Water."

She nodded, understanding flashing in her eyes. "Still," she said. "You can't let that hold you back. You two are incredible together."

I couldn't argue with her on that note, either.

I sucked in a sharp breath, smiling at her. "You're right. And I don't need to think about this now. Not today. Not when this is such a huge day."

Echo smiled. "True," she said. "You've earned every inch of this success, lady. Time to celebrate it."

I grinned. "With punch instead of drinks," I said, playfully wrapping my arm around her.

"You can drink," she said, rubbing a hand over her tummy. "I'll have just as much fun watching you loosen up."

"Ha!" I shook my head. "I'm perfectly happy in solidarity with you." I hooked our arms together as we walked. "I'm so happy you're here," I admitted, silently thanking the fates for bringing us back together after a slight blip in our friendship from when she'd entered into a world I couldn't possibly follow.

"Me too," she said, squeezing my hand, her eyes saying she knew exactly what I was thinking. She blinked away some moisture in her eyes, as did I, and then she straightened. "Now," she said, her voice firm. "Let's go catch up to those Reaper boys and give Connell hell for how wrapped around your finger he is, showing up in an ostrich costume and all."

I laughed, and we increased our pace, heading toward the boys who would no doubt finish long before us. Heading toward a family I never knew I wanted, but a future I couldn't help but hope for.

13

CONNELL

"Ye ready for this?" I asked her as our driver told us we were two cars away from the red carpet.

"I think so," Annabelle said with a nervous smile.

"Ye look brilliant." She looked so perfect I didn't even want to kiss her for fear that it would mess up her make-up. Her red dress was a strapless number that showed off her incredible breasts and hourglass figure, but with her hair up in whatever twist-thing that was, her neck was a bigger temptation than I could resist. I leaned down and kissed the soft skin just beneath her jaw, and she murmured her appreciation.

"None of that right now, thank you," she said with a laugh. "It took me two hours and two stylists to look like this. I thought Langley was crazy when she called and offered, but I'm so glad I went with the other girls to get ready."

"You're beautiful every day, but I'm not arguing with that dress."

She flashed me a smile that turned my heart over. God, but the lass was beautiful.

"Walk me through it one more time," she begged as we moved forward.

"First, I'll get out of the car, and then I'll help you out," I told her as I took her hand.

"You won't let me fall? Because so help me God, if those cameras catch me—"

I cut her off by brushing a light kiss over her cherry red lips. She'd promised that it was the kind of lipstick that didn't rub off, but I honestly didn't care if it did. I'd have a clown mouth all night if it meant I got to kiss her.

"I won't let you fall," I promised. "Press will want to take a few pictures of us together, and then I'll probably have to do one or two singles. You can either wait for me right there or go inside—whatever makes you more comfortable."

We moved forward in line again, which meant it was our turn.

"Okay," she said with a nod. "Let's do this."

Squeezing her hand one last time, I let her fingers go and put on my public face. The door opened, and I stepped out to the roar of fans. This black-tie gala wasn't just for the Reapers. Celebrities and politicians had all come out to help raise funds for the Children's Hospital.

I waved to the crowd, then turned for Annabelle.

"Pivot, feet down," I heard her mutter as she turned in the seat. Her heeled feet appeared, and then she took my hand and stood.

"Beautiful," I said softly into her ear as we walked down the first part of the carpet. I tucked her hand into the crook of my elbow to make sure that she stayed steady. She'd never get over it if she tripped, even a little bit.

Her smile was as radiant as she was, and even though I

felt her nerves in the tension of her muscles, she never let the fans see it. She looked calm, poised, and so very happy.

God knew my grin was huge for that same reason.

"Connell!" Some of the photographers called out as we made it to the backdrop section of the entry.

I switched my grip on Annabelle, winding my arm around her so I could tuck her into my side. We smiled for everyone who demanded our attention.

"This is wild," she said while the cameras clicked away.

I looked down at her, and our eyes met. "It's a hell of a lot more fun with you here, that's for sure."

"You sure? I mean, I did draw the line at the ostrich costume." Her smile was wide and bright as she dusted my tux's lapel.

"We would have made a statement," I argued as the clicks raged on.

"The wrong one," she countered. "Tonight is about how incredible *you* are, not Sweet Water. You deserve this. You're amazing."

We turned back to the cameras and smiled for a few more pictures, then kept walking down the carpet.

"Solo time," she said with a pat of my arm. "I'll be right up there." She motioned toward the end of the reporter gauntlet.

"I'll be there as soon as I possibly can," I promised with a kiss on her cheek.

Damn if she didn't look just as good walking away as she did right next to me.

"Connell! A few questions?" A reporter called out.

And so it began.

"We're a few weeks into the season, and we're wondering how you feel the Reaper's chances for the Cup this year," the first one asked.

"Well, it's only October, so there are a lot of games to play before we can even begin to think about playoffs. But I will say that we have a great team this year, and I have the highest of hopes."

I answered questions about the new goalie and the other rookies, along with the few trades we'd taken and lost. The next reporter wanted to know about the ostrich costume. The next asked about the charitable fund.

On and on the questions went until it had at least been ten minutes since Annabelle left my side.

Finally, I reached the last reporter.

"Hi, Connell!" the perky blonde said with a wave.

"Hey there." I smiled, glad that this was the last of them.

"I'm Penny Whitmore with Charleston Chatter, and our readers are just dying to know about these rumors that you're dating a local girl." She held out the microphone.

"They're not rumors. I'm in a relationship with a beautiful, smart woman from Sweet Water." My smile turned real at the thought of Annabelle.

"That's what we thought! So since it's just the two of us—"

Two of us my arse.

"Does this mean you're turning over a new leaf? You've been one of the Reapers' most eligible bachelors since you moved to Charleston last year, and though we've heard many southern girls have tried to win your heart, you just weren't a relationship guy! Does this mean that there's hope for your many fans that you might be looking local?"

I blinked and tried to keep my smile in place.

"I would have to say that I was waiting for the right girl. I think the right woman can make any man ready for a relationship. But as for looking local, I'd have to say no, since I've already found Annabelle."

Penny Whitmore's forehead puckered. "Oh. So—" her eyes darted sideways, "so you're in this for the long haul?"

"I am," I confirmed. "Why do you seemed so surprised?" My smile flattened.

"Oh, well, we do this segment every week where we compare celebrity relationships, and when we compared pictures of you with past flames to pictures with you and...Annabelle, we noticed that she definitely doesn't blend in with your usuals."

You're on film. Keep it polite. Langley will crush your balls if you give this woman a real piece of your mind.

I swallowed and composed my words carefully.

"She definitely isn't my usual type," I admitted. "She made me chase her relentlessly for one. I can't ever remember having to work so hard to get a date in my entire life." I laughed, trying to lighten the interview. "Truthfully, in the past, I've always dated women who were in the same social sphere. Women who were used to this kind of thing." I gestured down the carpet. "And Annabelle is refreshingly new to all of this. So when ye note that she's not my usual type, I absolutely agree with you. I'm used to women at my level, and Annabelle is completely and totally out of my league. I have no idea why she puts up with me, honestly."

Ms. Whitmore's jaw dropped, and she struggled to recover. "Lucky girl."

"I'm the lucky one. Trust me. Now, if you'll excuse me, we have money to raise." I gave her a smile that wasn't in the least bit friendly and turned to see Annabelle only a few feet away.

By the mix of awe and happiness on her face, she must have heard what I'd just said.

I reached for her, and she placed her hand in mine.

"That..." She shook her head as her words failed.

"I know ye don't want to hear it, but I love ye. And every word I said was true. Ye are entirely out of my league. But I'm thankful you're willing to date down a wee bit." I brushed a kiss across her forehead, and then we were moving.

We walked past the doormen and into the event, which

was decorated in lush shades of green and gold. My girl stood out just like she should have.

"So, what do we do now?" Annabelle asked, looking into the crowd milling before us.

"You both look fabulous!" Persephone said with her sugar-sweet drawl as she approached in a pale blue ballgown that reminded me of a Disney movie. "Annabelle, you make that dress a knockout, and thank you for talking Connell out of that ostrich suit he wore to your 5K."

"Thank you!" Annabelle answered. "And really, I can't thank you enough for all you did getting the Reapers to the 5K, and coming yourself! This..." Annabelle looked over the decor as the band took the stage. "This is just lovely. You're so talented!"

Persephone blushed, ducking her head slightly as a tall, thin man came up behind her, putting his hand on the small of her back.

"You should have seen our senior prom. This woman sure knows how to plan a party," he said. "Michael Carlisle," he introduced himself with an outstretched hand.

"Connell MacDhuibh," I answered, "And this is my girl-friend, Annabelle Clarke."

"Lovely to meet you," Annabelle said as her gaze flickered between the two of them.

"Michael is an old friend of my family," Sephie said with a slightly strained smile.

"We've known each other since we were in diapers. If this was the Middle Ages, our parents would have signed the betrothal papers years ago." He laughed.

"But it's not, thank goodness." Sephie swallowed. Then she looked past me, and her eyes widened.

"Well, it really is beautiful in here," Annabelle said to ease the awkward moment. "And you look gorgeous!"

But Sephie's eyes were now on the man standing next to me.

"Ye made it!" I said to Cannon. "And you're even dressed up. Did ye lose a bet?" I'd never seen the man in a tux. He'd skipped out on every fundraiser that required he wear anything dressier than jeans.

He didn't answer. I wasn't sure if it was because he was being his normal surly-self, or if he was distracted by the petite blonde. Either way, it got bloody awkward quickly.

"Cannon." Sephie's voice was light.

"Persephone." Cannon's wasn't.

I wasn't the only one who picked up on the energy. Michael-whatever looked between the two and narrowed his eyes slightly.

"Sephie, why don't we dance before your evening gets too busy?" he asked, stepping even closer to her. "It looks like the band is about ready to start."

Oh look, now there was another silent pause. This would have been almost comedic if it wasn't so bloody tense. A muscle in Cannon's jaw ticked, and I mentally calculated how quickly I could put myself between him and the prissy guy.

"Sure," Sephie finally agreed, still looking at Cannon. "I appreciate you coming. I know this is usually something you'd avoid."

"It's for sick kids."

"I'm still grateful."

The band started playing, but the awkward tension didn't dissipate.

"Sephie, that's our cue," Michael suggested.

"Right. I'll see you guys later," she said to Annabelle and me and then turned back to Price. "Cannon."

"Persephone."

She walked away with Michael's hand on her back, but she shook it off before they got too far.

"So that was inter—" I started.

"Who the fuck was that prick?" Cannon growled.

"A friend of her family," Annabelle answered.

His jaw ticked again.

"It seemed like she wasn't into him if that makes you feel better?" I glanced over at my very tall, very tatted, very out of place friend.

"Why the fuck would I care about who she's into?" He stalked off, heading toward a table of brunettes.

"Well, that was…" Annabelle tilted her head.

"Awkward? Weird? Downright odd?"

"I was going to say full of sexual tension." She shrugged.

"What?"

"Oh come on, those two should be smoking a cigarette after all that eye-sex." She gestured toward where Persephone danced with Michael. "Now, let's get out there."

Just like that, my broody friend was forgotten, and I had Annabelle in my arms as the band changed songs to *Wonderful Tonight.*

"You did great out there," I told her as we swayed back and forth on the floor.

"You were incredible," she said, looking up at me and cupping the back of my neck. "You really meant all that, didn't you? The stuff about being the lucky one?"

"Aye. Because I am. Remember, it was me chasing ye, not the other way around, Annabelle." I pulled her closer until our bodies moved together as one.

She shook her head with a soft smile. "I keep waiting for the other shoe to drop."

I brushed my lips over hers. "There's no other shoe. There's just ye and me and whatever we decide to make of this. I know your past. I know you're worried about my schedule, and I hate being separated from ye. I really do. But we've already made it through one away series, and it wasn't too bad, was it?"

"Because you stayed in your hotel room and facetimed with me instead of going out with your friends." She arched a delicate brow at me.

"True, but I did exactly what I wanted to do. If I couldn't be with you in person, I had the next best thing."

"You can't always do that," she lectured as the floor around us filled with other dancing couples. "You have to go out with your friends. You can't become the Reaper Recluse because you're worried that I'll worry. I trust you."

"Good, because I love ye. And I'm sure I'll go out with the guys, but it was our first away series, and I wanted to make sure you..." I tried to think of words that wouldn't get me into a fight.

"Didn't freak out?" she suggested with a wide smile.

"Can I plead the fifth? Or do you have to be an American citizen to do that?"

She laughed, and I turned and dipped her, holding her parallel to the floor as I kissed her. It was soft and sweet, and still enough to set me on fire. She was enchanting—that was the best word I had to describe her. Bewitching. Beguiling.

I brought her upright, and her eyes fluttered open as she smiled up at me. "Thank you for tonight."

"Thank ye for all of it." I kissed her again, uncaring of who was watching or taking photos. The reporter had one thing right. I was in this for the long haul. If I was this crazy for the woman after only a few months, I wondered how big it would feel in a few years.

I had every intention of finding out.

14

ANNABELLE

"*I* don't believe I've ever seen him smile," I said, motioning to Cannon across the party, leaning not so casually in a darker corner, his dark eyes tracking every movement, but he wasn't really *participating* in the party's festivities. Not since his arrival and that intense exchange, anyway.

"I did once," Connell said from my side. "His nose was in a book though, and I didn't dare tell him I saw it."

I smiled. "Well, that's adorable."

Connell cocked a brow at me, squeezing me where his hand rested on my hip. "Cannon Price is not adorable," he practically growled.

I pinched his side. "I meant that you didn't give him hell over it. I love books too, and sometimes people can be real jerks about what you choose to read."

He planted a chaste kiss on my lips. "Have I told you look beautiful tonight?"

A flush swept over my skin. "Several times, thank you."

And he looked down-right delectable in his suit—the way

it shaped his body, the way it made his blue eyes ten times *more* blue. It should be illegal to look as good as he did.

"How about some champagne?" he asked, motioning toward the bar across from the dancefloor.

"Love some," I said, my hand easily slipping into his as he led us to the bar. He settled me on the lone available barstool, electing to stand behind me as he ordered our drinks.

"Connell MacDhuibh," a sultry voice with a British accent called from behind us.

I turned to see, as did Connell, who smiled wide at the woman standing before him. She had gorgeous red hair that hung in waves to her shoulders, green eyes, and a slender figure evident from the slip of a gown she wore. She somehow looked sexy and elegant in the most effortless way.

"Ginger Levenson," Connell said, his hand slipping from mine to give the woman a generous hug. "What the hell are ye doing here?"

She patted him on the back before they broke apart, Connell's back still to me. My stomach twisted, unsure if I should stand up and introduce myself or spin my body back toward the bar and pretend like I didn't exist.

"In the States for a shoot," she said. "Snagged an invite. Rumor in the social circles is that Persephone Vandoren throws the grandest events." She glanced around the elaborate party. "Rumors, for once, did not disappoint."

Connell nodded, but quickly turned around, slipping his arm around my shoulders. "Ginger, this is my lady Annabelle," he said, and the tension in my chest instantly melted at the way his accent rolled over the titled he'd appointed me. "Annabelle, this is an old friend of mine, Ginger Levenson."

I reached my hand out, shaking hers briefly. "Nice to meet you," I said.

A partygoer vacated the barstool next to me, and Ginger

instantly sat down. "Thank the stars," she said. "These heels are treacherous, but I promised my agent I'd wear them." She pointed to the black pumps she wore.

I laughed, showing her mine. "Completely understand."

"Connell!" Logan called from where he stood with a few other Reapers near the silent auction tables. "Come here," he said, waving Connell over.

Connell leaned down and kissed my cheek before hurrying off the see what Logan needed. I scanned the crowd for Blaire, assuming she couldn't be far away. I spotted her across the room near the facilities, laughing with a drink in her hand as she chatted with one of the NFL players that had been on Persephone's invite list—a brother of a Reaper...Nathan Noble, if my memory was correct. And Hudson Porter's brother—an MLB star—chatted with Hudson not four feet from them. The building was packed full of so much celebrity testosterone it was a wonder a fight hadn't broken out yet. Though, I doubted anyone would dare to cross Persephone, not when she had connections in every major social circle from here to the west coast.

"So, you're the new lady in Connell's life, yeah?" Ginger asked, her nails clinking against the glass tumbler the bartender had placed in front of her.

I took a fast sip of my champagne. "Yes," I said, confident in my answer. We were together, we were exclusive, and I was *so* over doubting our relationship at every turn.

"That's nice," she said, but she pressed her lips into a line. "But, I would feel awful if I didn't warn you."

I straightened on the barstool, tilting my head.

"We dated for a bit," she admitted. "Years ago." She laughed at something I was completely oblivious to but continued on. "And it was never enough."

"What do you mean?"

"Me. I was never enough. Despite how we got along," she

said. "He constantly needed more. More laughs. More attention. More exposure for his career." She sighed. "It was exhausting." There was nothing malicious in her tone or in the way she looked at me, nothing but sincerity. "I don't know how deep you're in yet," she said after taking a quick drink. "But I couldn't *not* say anything. I'd hate for you to end up like I did, not feeling like you're enough to sustain him."

I checked myself internally. Remembered the words Connell had told the reporter earlier. My heart swelled with a solid, strong sense of truth, and I smiled at her. "I appreciate the warning," I said. "But I think you knew a different Connell."

She pursed her lips, a slight hint of pity flickering there, but it couldn't touch me.

She didn't know him. Not anymore. And honestly, it sounded like she never had. Because him needing more laughs had nothing to do with a need for attention and everything to do with a deep-seated drive to lift spirits and lighten the mood. To clear the darkness from any situation because that is what he'd spent the first part of his life doing and he didn't know another way to live.

"Maybe," Ginger said, and I finished my champagne, setting the empty glass on the bar.

"It was nice meeting you," I said as I crossed the room, my heart full and soaring and pounding with the absolute adoration I had for the man I headed toward.

A newfound sense of energy pulsed through my blood, my soul, and weaved together to create one unbreakable force. My head spun with the knowledge of it, with the release I felt at finally allowing myself to let go.

"Sorry, love," Connell said the moment I reached him. "Logan is bidding on the European getaway, and he wanted to know if the locations were shite or not."

"No need to be sorry," I said, waving him off. I couldn't

stop the smile on my lips as I looked at him, *really* looked at him with clear eyes and a free and open heart.

"You're brilliant," he whispered in my ear, his thumb grazing my bottom lip. "That smile kills me," he said.

I reached up to meet his ear. "Want to explore the penthouse?" I whispered, sinking back to my level.

His blue eyes sparked.

"I mean," I said. "Only if you're done with the party. We can stay—"

He smiled and shook his head, a few of his blond strands falling across his forehead. He intertwined our fingers and tugged us across the ballroom, through friends and strangers alike, until we reached the elevator.

The doors had barely slid shut before his hands snaked around my waist, hauling me against him. I arched my neck, ready to taste his kiss, but he lingered, hovering just above my mouth, his eyes on mine.

My heart beat furiously against my chest, so hard I'm sure he could feel it. Electricity buzzed between us, a white-hot current that pulsed and sizzled, and my stomach flipped with nerves. With need. With the firm realization that *this* moment was different than all the others.

The way his eyes churned with a sincerity and vulnerability I'd never seen before, he felt it too.

With a feather-light tenderness, he brushed his lips over mine. Soft, smooth, sweet. Nothing to match the hunger humming in our bodies, but gentle enough to bring tears to my eyes. To storm my soul with the emotions I'd let loose from the cage I'd kept them in for far too long.

The elevator dinged and the doors slid open, Connell not missing a beat as he swept an arm under my knees and carried me into the incredibly large room. The city skyline twinkled outside the floor-to-ceiling windows framing the living room, but he passed the area and easily navigated us to the bedroom. The place was big enough to fit two of my master bedrooms in it, and the bed was a luxurious pile of down and silk.

Connell held me, those eyes on mine as he grinned at me, savoring the slow pace he'd set, the burn between us both.

I reached up, kissing him tenderly before pulling back, my breath catching in all that built in my chest.

"You're trembling, love," he said, noticing the way I slightly shook against him. My nerves twisting and firing in all sorts of ways.

I laughed nervously, biting my lip to ground my mind.

"I love you." The words flew past my lips on a breath I felt I'd been holding for as long as I could remember.

His eyes flared, and he crushed his mouth on mine, and I felt his sigh of relief in every inch of my body. "I love you, Annabelle," he said between kisses. "I love ye so damned much."

My heart soared at the words, at the way I felt in his arms —safe and desired, and like nothing else existed or mattered beyond *this*.

We pulled apart, our chests heaving with ragged breath, and we *laughed*.

Laughed from the freedom in the truth of our admission. In the soaring sensation of falling. Laughed because of the happiness swarming us both.

And then he shifted, sliding me down every inch of his body to set me on my feet, and I gasped at the heat between my thighs. At the hardness begging for release from his tight dress pants.

But he didn't rush.

No, he took his time, kissing down the seam of my neck, my shoulder as he lowered one dress strap, then the other. He slowly spun me, his lips raising flames as he trailed them down my spine as he unzipped my dress until it was a puddle of silk at my feet. He held my hand as I carefully stepped out of it, my black heels still strapped around my ankles. The blue in his eyes turned to liquid flame as he trailed the length of my body, pausing at the scrap of black lace covering my center. At the strapless bra and my breasts threatening to spill out of the cups.

"Brilliant," he said, wetting his lips, and I trembled from the hunger in his appraisal.

I took a step toward him, my hands sliding up his hard chest until I reached his top button. I made quick work of removing his dress jacket and shirt, my lips and teeth teasing the bare skin of his abdomen as I worked my way lower. He hissed as I dropped to my knees, removing his pants and boxer-briefs, and I flicked my tongue over his thick head on my way back to standing.

"Brilliant, cruel woman," he said, tangling his fingers in my hair as he pulled me against him. He held his mouth a breath from mine and tugged my hair. I arched my neck, completely at his mercy.

"Beautiful, hilarious man," I teased, the motion of my words making our lips nearly touch. "I love you," I said again because I couldn't keep it contained.

The words were his undoing because one second he held us in agonizing anticipation and the next? He was sliding his hands down my hips, hooking them under my ass to haul me up and up until I had to lock my ankles around his waist. I kissed him hungrily, greedy with needing to taste him.

He squeezed my ass as he held me against him, fucking my mouth with his tongue in sweeping strokes that told me exactly where he intended this night to go. A quick nibble on my bottom lip and he laid me on the bed. He smirked that wickedly mischievous grin of his before hooking his hands behind my knees and hauling my ass to the edge of the bed. He walked his fingers up my thighs until he reached the hem of my panties and slid them over my high heels, tossing the lace over his shoulder.

The man dropped to his knees, and the sight of him there, the hunger in his eyes as he settled my legs over his strong shoulders—it was enough to draw a whimper from my lips.

Then he set his mouth on me, and stars burst behind my eyes. The sensation of his lips on my slick flesh, his *tongue*, teasing, flicking, thrusting in and out of me. I arched into him, fisting the fabric beneath me, holding on as he pushed me farther and farther toward that sweet edge. The one that bordered on ecstasy and pain. The one that I never knew existed before him. The one that I was nearly sure he *invented*. Because he owned me, body and soul, and god damn he knew how to make me sing for him.

My thighs clenched on his shoulders as feasted on me, switching from sweet and slow to hard and fast like he simply couldn't get enough of the taste of me in his mouth. The thought spiraled me higher, wound me tighter until I was a coiled spring of heat and gasps and *need*.

"Connell!" I moaned his name as I writhed beneath him, his arm keeping me firmly in place as he continued to lick and suck at me until I couldn't see straight. Until I wasn't sure I'd ever escape this feeling—all tight and loose at the same time.

And then he flattened his tongue against that bundle of nerves, rocking his head up and down until I shattered around his mouth completely. A cry loosened from my lips as I arched off the bed.

Connell stood, his eyes wild in a primal way as he licked his lips. "Delicious," he said, his voice rough, low.

I panted, my arms limp at my sides, my knees trembling.

Connell snaked one arm underneath my hips, holding me in a raised position off the bed while my upper back remained against the mattress. His other hand guided my legs up and up until my calves rested against his shoulders. Until his hard cock teased the slickness between my thighs.

He gripped my hips, content to tease me with his thick head, slipping in an inch and then quickly pulling back.

Torture.

Pure, delicious torture.

"Connell," I chided, completely at his mercy in this position.

He smirked. "Annabelle."

"Please," I said through clenched teeth when he'd slipped in again only to pull right back out.

"Please what?"

"Fuck me," I nearly growled the words, and he *laughed*. Laughed that confident laugh that caressed every inch of my skin.

"Like this?" He plunged all the way inside me, and I arched my head against the mattress, fisting the fabric again at the pleasure rippling my body as he filled me.

"Yes!" I said on a tight breath.

"This?" he asked again, pulling out completely before thrusting in to the hilt.

"God, yes," I said as he did it again.

He kept a firm hold on my hips, in full control of my body, my heart, as he thrust in again and again and again. The angle allowed him to go deeper, harder than ever before, and he filled me so much I couldn't think or *breathe* around the feel of him. Of the way he hit that spot deep inside me, the one that sparked for him, the one that made my entire body tremble, the one that made my head spin with pleasure.

And I could do nothing but watch him fuck me, own me. The sight of this man...this beautiful, strong man taking his fill of my body, my soul, *God* it made release barrel down my spine. Made a cry burst from my lips as I clenched around his hard, hot length inside me. Made my entire body come alive as one orgasm rolled right into another as he thrusted, over and over again until my body sparked and buzzed with a weeping energy I couldn't contain. Until waves of pleasure consumed me, body and mind. And then he hardened to the nth degree inside me and threw his head back, a deep groan rumbling from his chest as he found his own release, drawing one last burst from me along with him.

I could barely draw breath as we came down, as he gently slid out of me, resting my legs back on the bed, and quickly, sweetly cleaned us up. He settled behind me on the bed, encasing me in his arms as we both slowed our racing hearts. As we laid in the silence of our passions, the air crackling with the intensity of it all. And as my eyelids grew heavy, my head resting against his chest, something settled in my soul. A kind of security and love I'd never known. And I whispered the words one more time before my body succumbed to the utter exhaustion Connell had wrung from it.

15

CONNELL

"You must be exhausted." Annabelle's voice came through my phone, bringing waves of homesickness with it. We were at the end of a three-game away series, and I was fitting in a photoshoot for my new Armani endorsement.

"I am," I admitted as I looked out my hotel room window. "But I know how lucky I am, too, so it cuts the whining down. What are you up to today?"

"Paperwork," she said with a sigh. "Lacy already took off for an early lunch."

I laughed. "I thought she was supposed to outgrow that whole newlywed phase? Or could it be that you're less annoyed than you let on and more jealous that I'm not home to take you to an early lunch?"

"Definitely the second. You're coming home the day after tomorrow, right?"

"That's the plan. I have the photoshoot here in a few minutes, and then I agreed to a magazine interview. Then it's straight over to the game." God, I wished I was headed home tonight. I couldn't wait to slide into bed next to her. Not just for the sex, though that was definitely a bonus, but just to hold her.

"I know you'll do great."

"I wish ye were here." Some of the players traveled with their wives or girlfriends, from time to time, but Annabelle's career came first, and I respected that.

"Me, too. But just think. When you get home, I'll be in bed waiting for you. That should keep you going for the next two days."

I sighed. "That's enough to put me on the next plane."

She laughed. "Two more days. Your house or mine?"

"I'll go wherever ye are." It was true, and didn't just apply to where we slept.

"In that case, I'll be at your house. I bet you've missed your bed."

"I've missed *ye*." A knock sounded on my door. "Aye?"

"Mr. MacDhuibh? We're ready for you." The voice was slightly muffled through the door.

"I'll be there in just a minute," I called back. "I guess it's time to go smile for a bit."

"What are you wearing?" Her teasing tone brought an immediate grin to my lips.

"A full suit. Tie and all. Don't worry, I won't be half-naked or anything."

She laughed. "I don't mind if you're half-naked in an advertising campaign. It's okay if other women ogle you. I know who you come home to."

"Aye, that ye do. Gotta run. I love ye."

"I love you."

Those three words slid over me like a balm, soothing the ache in my chest that had been there since I'd left Charleston days ago. I'd never minded being away for extended times before, but I'd also never had someone to go home to like I did now.

We hung up and I walked out of my suite to see two women with clipboards. "I'm ready."

"Perfect," one said, barely looking up from her board. "Mr. MacDhuibh, we're ready for you right across the hall. I'm Sherry, and I'll be here to take care of whatever you need." She looked up and nodded. "It fits well."

"Should be, since ye had it made custom," I said with a slight smirk, fingering the tie I'd negotiated for the shoot—a gift from Annabelle.

"It looks phenomenal," the other woman said, her voice leaving the sphere of professional.

"Vanessa," Sherry chastised.

"Sorry, I'm just a really big fan," Vanessa said.

"Not a problem," I said with a smile that was kind, but wouldn't encourage the lass.

They led me across the hall into another suite that had been transformed for the photo shoot. The backdrop was simple and white, and ample staff scurried about, getting everything perfect.

"Mr. MacDhuibh," the photographer greeted me. "It's a pleasure to work with you. We'll get you out of here as soon as possible. We know you have a game tonight."

"Thank ye." It was the last time I spoke for a while.

They took pictures for the next ten minutes. Sitting, standing, leaning against the wall. All of it. Then they brought in the women. Models flanked me, all wearing barely-there gowns in bright, solid colors.

They were professional, and the shoot was easy.

"Okay, now for the wardrobe change," the photographer ordered with a snap of his fingers. "Mr. MacDhuibh, you look great. I know we're running behind schedule, but once we have this next series we should be done. The marketing director wanted both the classic shots and a few sexier ones."

"No problem," I said with a nod, then guzzled a bottle of

water. I nearly spit it out when the models came back, all in various colors and styles of lingerie.

Bloody hell. I'd told Annabelle that I wouldn't be half-naked, but I hadn't thought about the models. They were more like three-quarters naked.

A blonde shot me a look that told me she'd be up for some bedroom time, and I quickly looked away. Last year, I would have taken her up on it, but the truth was I had zero interest now.

First, I would never hurt Annabelle like that. There wasn't an orgasm in this world that was worth losing her.

But second, I wasn't even tempted. It was a revelation, but the models weren't even appealing to me. They lacked Annabelle's lush curves. Their smiles were plastic and even their laughs were fake.

Annabelle was genuine in every emotion. She was real in every way. She was the kind of woman to build a life with. The kind to stand by you in the sun and the storm.

I grinned as the models flanked me on either side because this was about to be ridiculously easy. There was no sexual tension, no sly glances, no arousal. I may as well have been taking pictures with my teammates.

And speak of the devil, Logan and Cannon stood off to the side, both looking rather impatient.

"That's great," the photographer praised the girls who posed. "Connell, let's go a little more serious? Maybe a smolder?"

"You should be doing this," I teased Logan, who had been born with the face for this shit.

"Hell no. Never happening." Logan shook his head.

"Smolder faster, MacDhuibh. We have a game to get to, just in case you've forgotten." Cannon ordered dryly.

"Mr. MacDhuibh, the magazine reporter is here for his

interview, too," Sherry said with a grimace. "I'm so sorry that we're behind schedule."

"Jesus, it's not like he needs his brain for the shoot. Just have him answer the fucking questions now," Cannon snapped.

Sherry took one look at the tattoos that crept up his neck and stepped back.

"That would be fine, Sherry. Would you mind bringing him in?" I asked.

Logan shook his head at Cannon. "Man, stop scaring off the women. No wonder you're single."

"Women who are scared off by some ink and a growl aren't worth my time. And I'm not after a relationship like you and the Scot. I'm quite happy rotating my bed partners."

A brunette cocked her eyebrow at Cannon with a smile.

He gave her a once-over and nodded.

I sighed and looked back at the camera for more instructions from the photographer. I didn't really give a fuck that Cannon slept with whomever he wanted. What I cared about was the uneasy feeling that it was just a symptom of a much larger, self-destructive pattern. Cannon wasn't just the fastest skater on our team—or the NHL—he was a friend. A friend who would bring everyone down around him if that lit fuse in his eyes ever reached detonation.

"Mr. MacDhuibh!" the reporter said with a smile, taking out his recorder. "She said you wanted to tackle the interview while you're shooting?" He gave the models an appreciative glance.

"If that's okay, Mr. Perry?" A girl draped herself across my chest, and the smell of hairspray engulfed me.

"Sure! Call me John."

"John, call me Connell."

We shared a grin, and he shook his head. "Man, that's some job you have."

"It pays the bills," I said with a shrug.

"Connell, if you could turn to the side?" the photographer asked. "Yes, just like that. Desiree, lift your head a little, sweetheart? There, now look up at him."

Her blue eyes met mine, and we held the pose.

"Okay, now Connell, I want you to really channel desire into this shot. Put your hand at her lower back."

Her bare back, since she was only wearing a matching bra and panty set with matching garters and stockings. My hand splayed wide across her skin, and I wanted to apologize to her—not just for my hands, but for an industry that required she be in such getup outside her bedroom.

"It's okay," she assured me, gripping the lapels of my suit.

"Do I look that uncomfortable?"

"Kind of." She crinkled her nose. "I'm fine. You're fine. And this is way more than I was wearing in the last Vickie's shoot."

"Right. Good to know."

"Connell, you look a little…" The photographer faded off.

"Like you're holding your sister," Cannon suggested.

Awesome.

"You have a girlfriend, right?" Desiree asked, looking up at me with fake lust in her eyes.

"Aye." One that would be anything but happy if she saw how I was holding this model.

"Just pretend I'm her. Close your eyes. Picture her, open them and keep that feeling. It's one or two clicks at most." She nodded supportively.

"Okay." I closed my eyes and pictured Annabelle in that sundress, up on her kitchen counter. Annabelle naked above me in my shower with her head thrown back as I licked her to an orgasm. Annabelle riding astride me, her eyes glazed and her lips parted.

Then I opened my eyes and focused on the area just above

the girl's eyes so the blue color didn't completely fuck me up when all I wanted was deep, soft brown.

I heard the clicks and prayed he got what he wanted.

"Perfect. Okay, reset," the photographer ordered.

The girls walked away for a second, and John came over. "Man, that's intense. You ever tap any of that? Off the record, of course."

"No," I replied as I was moved into the center of the backdrop by an assistant with a light meter.

"Right. Okay, so on the record?"

"Still the same answer."

John shook his head. "No, I meant, are you ready to start the interview? You know the feel of our magazine—very stylish. Very masculine."

"I've read it."

"Good. This issue is on success in sports. Basically a look at what makes you tick, what makes the long hours worth it."

"Fire away," I said as the girls finished doing whatever they were doing.

He started off asking about our hours, the away game schedules, and our pay. He moved on to the cars, the houses, and the women.

Ten minutes, a new suit, and what felt like thousands of pictures later, I grew impatient.

"Here's the thing," I told him as the models moved poses again. "Those questions might have really applied to me when I was in Miami, but the Reapers are a very...different atmosphere. Sure, we all have the nice cars and the great salaries. We're all lucky to do what we love for a living. But it's a much more family-centered team. Most of us live in the same neighborhood, and you don't see the same...flash that I have on other teams."

"And the women?" he asked as the girls flanked me for a group shot.

"I'm in a committed relationship with a woman I love and respect very much. A woman that I actually met because I'm a jackass, not because I'm a hockey player."

"And does she care that you have six Victoria's Secret models hanging off you right now?" He scanned the models with a grin.

"I'm sure it's not her favorite part of dating me," I answered truthfully. "But she trusts me with good reason. And from what I've seen, these lovely women are highly professional."

It wasn't like we were having an orgy in front of the camera for fuck's sake.

"Right, but you have pretty much every man's dream job, and you spend your days like this—next to the women every woman in America wants to be, and every American man wants to fuck. Are you telling me that you don't...indulge?"

"I'm sorry?" My jaw locked.

"You guys are on the road so much, you must—"

Yeah, that was enough.

"Are you serious? First off, let's remember that I'm *not* American. Yeah, okay," I said in a mocking tone. "What, like we're all the same, right? Us NHL players. We all fuck around on the road because our relationships are only to keep our beds warm at home and raise our kids, and hey, it's not cheating if you're in a different area code. Isn't that the saying? I mean, what bampot could possibly resist all the beautiful women throwing themselves at us, right?" I glared at him.

"Something like that," he said with a nod.

"Something like...ye can fuck right off," I snapped. "You write for a highly respected men's magazine," I said, stepping away from the girls. "So have a little more respect for your audience. No, I don't cheat on my girlfriend. I only *indulge* in her. It does count as cheating if you're in a different area code, and I don't know a single Reaper who fucks around on his woman. We all have the self-control to walk away from available pussy because our women mean the entire world to us."

I turned to the models who all stood gawking. "Not that you ladies aren't lovely, but I happen to be madly in love with the woman I have waiting for me at home."

"Totally get it," Desiree said with a nod.

The brunette was already eyeing Cannon.

"So if we're done here?" I asked John.

"Yeah...okay. Thank you for your time. You were my last interview, so the digital article will be up tomorrow and the print will be out in a few weeks."

"I'm looking forward to it." Sarcasm practically dripped from my tone.

"Thanks. Uh, we still okay to use a couple of the shots?" he asked the photographer.

"Yeah, Armani is cool with it as long as you mention that it's from this shoot. I'll send you a few shots tonight."

John muttered his thanks and walked out.

The models behind me clapped. "That was awesome!" Desiree laughed.

"Okay, ladies, last shot!" The photographer ordered. "Connell, we need you to walk forward and girls you fall to the back. Yep, like that."

I stood in front of the camera with a delighted smirk on my face because I'd meant every word I'd said to that misogynistic prick.

The photographer started snapping, and then said, "Now!"

The girls opened fire, and I was hit with streams of cold, water...no...champagne? I laughed hard as they sprayed me down. The pranker had been good and pranked.

"And we're done!" The photographer announced.

An assistant—Vanessa—rushed at me with a soft towel, and I wiped the champagne off my face before drying my hair. "Sorry about that. We thought it might be more genuine if you didn't know it was going to happen."

"Quite alright," I assured her as I dripped champagne onto the floor.

"She's lucky, you know," she said quietly, looking up at me without the blatant invitation she'd broadcast earlier.

"She?" I asked, ridding myself of my soaked jacket.

"Your girlfriend. We do shoots like this a lot and...well, she's just really lucky." She took the towel and the jacket from me.

"I assure you, I'm the lucky one."

"And we will be the lucky ones if you get your ass out of that suit because we have a game!" Cannon shouted.

"Right. We have a game," I agreed with a grin.

And in a couple of days, I'd get to go home to Annabelle. It took exactly five minutes to get into the suit I'd actually wear over to the arena, and two of those were to shower the liquor off me.

"Why the hell are you still grinning like an idiot?" Cannon asked as we rode the elevator to the lobby.

"Just happy, I guess. The love of a good woman will do that for you, right, Logan?"

"True," he said, his eyes falling to his phone. "Speak of the devil. Hey, babe," he said as his phone lit up with the facetime call.

"For fuck's sake," Cannon muttered.

"Hey! Can you see me?" Blair waved.

"Give me a second, we're in the elevator."

The doors dinged, and Logan walked out ahead of us.

"Did you hear me? I got a Birkin bag!" She lifted some kind of satchel to the screen.

"That's nice," Logan said as we made our way through the lobby. "You having fun shopping in Atlanta?"

"Yeah, it's great! I still can't believe you sent me with your credit card!"

At that, Cannon and I shared a look. He gave her his fucking credit card?

"No problem."

"Babe, you don't get it. They don't just *give* these out. You can't even buy them unless you're *someone*." Good God, the woman sounded like she'd just been given the Holy Grail.

"That's...really great," Logan assured her in a placating tone.

"They weren't going to give one to me, but I happened to open my Instagram page while I was at the Hermes store and left it just...sitting there with a picture of you, and then the sales consultant noticed."

"Okay?" Logan's voice shifted a little as we walked outside where the bus waited.

Fuck, we were ten minutes late.

"So then she recognized you and when she realized we're together, she let me buy one! It was only like thirty-five, too!" She grinned.

"Thirty-five hundred? I don't know much about bags. Is that good?"

Coach stood outside the bus with crossed arms, looking anything but pleased.

"What? No, thirty-five thousand. You said I didn't have a limit, right? I mean, I'll take it back if you want me to, but...I'll *never* get another one. It would be so... But I'll take it back if that's what you want, babe."

"No. It's fine. You're right, I said there wasn't a limit. I'm just happy you're happy. But I have to get on the bus now, babe. Game tonight, remember?"

"Oh, that's right! Go win!" She made a kissing noise that I was more than happy to get away from as we got on the bus.

"Glad you decided that the game was as important as your photoshoot, Connell." Coach lifted a brow at me.

"Yeah, sorry about that one," I cringed.

"Get in your seats. All of you. Logan, get off the damned phone!"

I sat in the first empty seat I found, which was next to Sawyer. Then I pulled out my phone and texted Annabelle as we drove toward the rink.

Connell: Thank you for being you.

Annabelle: LOL. Who else would I be?

I thought about that call. About the way Blaire was blatantly using Logan's celebrity. At least she made him happy, though. Right?

Connell: I just love you.

Annabelle: I love you, my Scotsman.

Annabelle: Play hard tonight. And remember that I'll still do you if you lose.

I scoffed a laugh.

Connell: Good to know.

Annabelle: Now get home to me, would you?

Connell: Working on it, lass.

I put my phone away with a smile. "Is it harder now with away games, knowing that you have Echo?" I asked the kid to my left.

Like the four years between us made me old or something.

"Yeah," he answered with a nod. "But it makes going home even better knowing she's there."

"That's the truth." I'd never looked forward to going home so much in my life.

"She's crazy about you," Sawyer told me with a solemn look. "Annabelle."

168

"Thank God, because I'm crazy about her."

"Good. Because if something happens and you end up hurting her..." he shook his head.

"I know, you'll be honor bound to kick my ass. Don't worry, I'll let you get a few good punches in. But really, you don't have to worry. I love her. There's zero chance in this world I'd do anything to hurt Annabelle."

"Thank God, because it wouldn't be me kicking your ass, it would be Echo."

"That is a truly frightening thought."

"She is a truly frightening woman," he admitted with a smirk.

"Here's to loving best friends."

"May they never team up against us."

I laughed. "Now that would be terrifying."

"You two are giving me hives," Cannon muttered from across the aisle.

"Just wait until it's you," Sawyer said with a tip of his head.

Cannon shot us a look and buried his face in whatever his book of the day was.

Truth was, I'd had the same reaction to that sentiment months ago...before Annabelle. And now I couldn't imagine my life without her. She was a lightning strike that set my world on fire and changed *everything*.

Personally, I couldn't wait to watch that smug, sulking ass fall in love.

God help the girl.

16

ANNABELLE

"*L*ove the reserve, Ms. Clarke!"

I paused my shopping cart in the cereal aisle, turning to smile at George Tankard, the general manager of Sweet Water grocery.

"I'm so glad you're enjoying it, George," I said.

"My grandkids visited from Florida last weekend," he said. "I took them and they loved it. Said I have to take them every time they visit!"

"That's wonderful." My heart soared, pride filling my chest. The reserve was a wide success, already bringing in tourists from Charleston and beyond. I'd texted Connell yesterday with our first set of numbers, and he'd sent me a silly selfie to celebrate. The goofy photo was now the lock screen on my phone. It made me stupid-grin every time I saw it.

"I've got to check the stock in the back," George said. "But let me know if you need anything special ordered."

"Not this week, George," I said. "But thank you so much for the offer."

He nodded, and hustled past me. Sweet Water's lone

grocery store was well stocked but there were times I'd had to drive to Charleston to get a special item. George hated the idea and had offered to special order items for me ever since. City Clerk had its perks, or more likely, the small-town kindness of Sweet Water was to blame. Mercy, I loved this community.

I bit back my smile as I hunted for my favorite honey-flakes cereal. I was full of love these days. I couldn't remember a time I'd been happier, and I had been the youngest city clerk to ever be elected to Sweet Water. This feeling inside me now? It squashed that, a feat I once thought impossible.

I had thought many things were impossible before Connell crashed into my life.

Like sex being something I craved on a daily basis.

I laughed, recalling our conversation at the bar months ago. When I'd argued that I could always do it better myself, so why waste time with the emotional drama of a man? What *little* I'd known then.

Connell had known, of course.

Cocky Scotsman.

A warm chill soared over my skin at just how *wrong* I'd been. At just how much Connell had taught me over the last few months.

Not solely about sex and pleasure, either, but about *life*. About laughing and letting go and not taking things as seriously as I had. He'd loosened me up in a way I never knew I needed. And the friendship? Sweet mercy, that man made me laugh. And he listened, *really* listened instead of just waiting for me to stop talking. He cared, took an interest in what was important to me, and good lord the man could wear the hell out of a brown jumpsuit. And I mirrored his enthusiasm for digging deep to the roots of what was important to him too —a perfect balance between us.

I turned the corner, hunting for a loaf of bread, and smiling like an idiot.

I loved that man.

I wanted to marry that man.

The shock of the truth in *that* thought pulsed through me like a lightning strike. It was enough to pause my search for bread, and there was little I loved more than carbs.

My eyes glistened slightly, but I blinked the happy tears away and shook my head. It was way too soon to think about marriage, but I couldn't help it. I was tragically, helplessly in love with Connell.

I took a deep breath, slowing the giddy thoughts of our future together.

One step at a time.

A pang of loneliness hit me as I gathered the rest of my groceries. I hadn't seen him in days. Joy of away games. Though, the distance did create a sort of charged anticipation that buzzed the entirety of the separation. It made it that much sweeter when he came home.

Finally checking off each item on my list, I headed toward the registers, but Lacy darted into my path, her cart forgotten feet behind her. I tilted my head at her frantic look.

"Lacy?" I asked, rounding my cart to touch her shoulder. "Is everything all right? Don okay?" My heart raced at the pain in her eyes.

She opened her mouth, then shut it as she scanned my face.

"What is it?"

"You haven't seen it," she said, her voice cracking.

"Seen what?"

She pressed her lips together before shaking her head. "Nothing. Not…a thing. Let's get out of here."

I crossed my arms over my chest, suddenly feeling like the floor beneath my feet tilted.

"Lacy, what in the world is going on?" My patience left me, replaced with a hollowing panic I couldn't understand.

"I was just here to grab a few things, then Don messaged me a funny meme, and then that led to some unintentional scrolling through social media. And I saw...I read..." she huffed. "Then I saw *you* and figured you'd already read it... oh, Annabelle, I'm so sorry." She wrapped her arms around me, but I quickly shoved her off.

"Is someone in my family hurt?" I quickly asked. "Because I'm clearly oblivious to what you're talking about."

"Everyone is fine..." she said, eyes dropping to the cell phone in her hand.

I reached a palm toward her. "Show me."

She hesitated. "Let's go to your place first."

I rolled my eyes, snatching her cell from her. "Honestly, Lacy, I know you get wrapped up in social gossip but what could possibly merit this reaction—"

The floor completely dropped from beneath my feet, my stomach flying with it.

Because there, on her cell phone screen, was Connell. He stared at me from the website showing the *cover* of Charleston's top men's magazine, with the headline:

Defenseman for the Carolina Reapers, Connell MacDhuibh admits to infidelity and shallow standards for what he prefers in a woman.

I don't remember scrolling down to read the article, but suddenly there were words and my eyes were widening at the pictures of Connell with numerous, gorgeous women. In lingerie. In a hotel room. Models. Picture perfect social stars.

"This can't be right," I said as Lacy placed a supportive hand on my back. "They had to get these pictures from months ago. Years ago."

But no, *there* was the tie I'd given him last month.

My mouth went dry, my stomach churning with acid.

Lacy's cell trembled between my fingers as I read the article, read the quotes gathered from Connell himself. Read how he'd responded to questions about the romantic lifestyle of a Reaper.

"We all fuck around on the road because our relationships are only to keep our beds warm at home and raise our kids, and hey, it's not cheating if you're in a different area code. I mean, what bampot could possibly resist all the beautiful women throwing themselves at us, right?"

Fuck, it even sounded like him. Not the content that shredded my soul, but the *way* he worded it, I could almost hear his accent rolling around the words. Understood the Scottish slang word for idiot because he'd said it countless times before. Hear the confident and playful tone in his voice.

My eyes darted from the article and up, realizing I now had the attention of every single person in the grocery store —George, the cashier, the customers, the bag boy.

"I'm an idiot," I whispered more to myself, my heart pounding as I looked at Lacy, then past her.

Every single person looked at me with pity in their eyes.

Sweat slicked my palms, heat rushing up my neck and to my cheeks.

My entire body shook from the mortification, from the judgment in their eyes.

It's happening again.

Everyone saw it before you.

"Lacy," I said, my voice cracking as I barely held back the tears. "I…I have to go." I backed away from my cart, no longer caring about the contents inside.

"I know," she said, nodding. "I'll grab these." She nodded to my cart. "I'll bring them by in a few."

I nodded my thanks and sprinted out the glass doors,

tears already streaming from my eyes before I'd even gotten behind the wheel of my car.

By sheer will I made it home, and locked the door behind me, instantly slumping to the floor.

Connell had played me for a damned fool.

All the doubts I had, all the fears I'd expressed...he'd hushed them, shooed them away. Assured me with kisses and accent drenched words that they weren't merited.

And I'd been dumb enough to believe him.

Anger flared hot in my chest, not at him but at *me*.

Because *I* was the one who fell.

I was the one who allowed myself to love a man who couldn't possibly remain mine alone.

How could he? With the lifestyle he lived?

Like I'd said from the beginning.

Did he think I'd never find out? Did he care?

You know better.

Some deep, wounded voice in the back of my head argued for him, begged me to call him.

I clenched my cell in my hand, his number up and ready.

But I locked my screen, my heart aching at the photo there.

He should've been honest with me. I told him from the beginning we didn't need to be serious. We didn't need to push it that direction.

A summer convenience until the season started.

Well, it'd started now.

And he was gone, doing God knew what.

Disgust rolled through my body at the too-ready images that flashed in my mind—Connell and all those beautiful women. Did they laugh about me? Did they joke about the curvy woman who thought she held his love?

I raked my palms over my face, forcing the tears away.

. . .

HOURS LATER, long after Lacy had kindly dropped off my groceries and hugged me, I walked into *Scythe*.

The place was crammed wall-to-wall in customers draped in their Reaper best, the game up on all the TV screens. I ignored those, heading straight to the bar. I needed my best friend. Needed Echo to help me figure out what to do about the situation, but she was swamped with customers on the other end of the bar, so I took my seat and waited.

The second she was free, she hurried over to me. "Okay, this can't be true," she said, foregoing a greeting.

I'd texted her the links to all the articles before I'd come over.

"Pretty hard to deny, Echo." I sighed. "It *sounds* like him."

She furrowed her brow.

"I mean not what he said," I clarified. "That was an ugly shock." I swallowed hard. "But his voice. It's his."

"You have to call him," Echo said, and I gaped at her.

"I don't want to speak to him."

She rolled her eyes. "You need to confront him with this. Hear his side—"

"His side?" I cut her off. "You think I need to listen to him explain why he thinks cheating outside of zip codes isn't considered cheating? That I want to hear him explain that he prefers his women on the road rail-thin and easily tossed around?" I choked on the last words, and Echo immediately poured me a vodka tonic, sliding the glass in front of me.

I gulped the contents down in three swallows, using the time to collect my breath. I would *not* cry in public.

"I know, babe," Echo said, leaning close to me. "But it doesn't add up."

"Doesn't it?" I shook my head. "I said it from the start." I shrugged. "I'm more mad at myself for ever thinking differently. After Atlanta...I should've known better. Should have—"

"Hey!" a customer called from the end of the bar. "Can we get some drinks down here please!"

"Calm your tits, Stan!" Echo hollered back, and the old man pursed his lips at her. "Stay here," she said. "I'll be right back."

I nodded, fiddling with my now empty glass.

"Omi*god,* Annabelle." Blaire's voice sounded just before she squeezed past another bar-goer and settled in the seat next to me. "I saw it all over my feed on the plane ride home from Atlanta," she said, her hand on my back. "How are you handling this?"

I parted my lips, but no words escaped.

Obviously, I wasn't handling it too fucking well.

"That's okay," she said when I didn't answer. "This kind of thing happens a lot, and you are going to make him *pay.*" She raised her brows, her lips shaping like she'd sucked a lemon.

"What?" I asked.

"You *have* to go public," she said, setting her phone on the bar. "What have you collected on him? Anything we can use?"

I tilted my head. "Collected?"

She huffed. "Yeah, pictures. Records. Things he admitted to you about his past?"

I shook my head.

"You've been with him for this long and you didn't collect one single thing you could use against him if something like this happened?"

I gaped at her like she was from another planet.

She waved me off. "That's okay," she said. "Unfortunate, but we can make something up."

"Make something up?" I repeated like some sort of confused parrot.

"Yes. We'll come up with the best, most heart-wrenching story. Oh!" She smacked my shoulder. "We could say he bought your ostriches from the black market or something. People will *hate* him for that."

"No—"

"And then," she cut me off. "You can tell him you'll only retract the story if he pays you compensation for your time and pain."

"You're joking right?" I asked, looking from her and then back to Echo who made her way toward us.

"Like hell I am," she said. "You deserve to make him pay. Now, let's roll with this ostrich story, 'kay? Trust me, they'll hate him. His PR rep will totally tell him to pay you to take it down. It'll be magic." She reached for her cell on the bar, but Echo snatched it up first.

"Echo!" Blaire chided.

"I don't know where the fuck you get off spouting this poison to my friend, but you sure as hell aren't doing it in my bar." Echo glared at her.

Blaire narrowed her gaze. "Don't pretend like we aren't the same, Echo," she snapped. "You'd do the same thing if Sawyer did this to you."

Echo rolled her eyes.

"You would! We have to protect ourselves. These Reapers are primed for two things—heartbreak and fame."

"And we can clearly tell which one you value most, you piece of trash." Echo tossed Blaire's cell at her chest, and she scrambled to catch it. "Get the fuck out of my bar."

Blaire opened her mouth to protest but Echo cut her off with a raised brow. Blaire raised her chin, spun off the chair, and stomped out of the bar.

I turned to Echo, my eyes wide. "Poor Logan."

Echo shook her head. "Doubt he even knows."

"*I* didn't know," I said. "She's always been nice to me."

"Well," Echo said, leaning against the bar. "Shit like this shows people's true colors."

I nodded.

"So, what are you going to do?" she asked, her voice softer in the loud bar.

My heart, what was left of the broken pieces, cringed at the question. I wanted to call Connell. Wanted him to tell me it was all a lie, but my survival instincts had kicked in the moment I read the article. The moment I saw the pity and judgment in everyone's eyes as they witnessed my downfall. My walls rebuilding, reinforcing. Pulling the pieces of myself back together so I could withstand this heavy a fallout.

"Can I have another drink?" I asked instead of answering her.

She sighed, but gave me a generous pour.

I scooped up the glass, raising it to her in thanks, and in a silent pledge to sit here and drink until I could no longer feel the pain.

17

CONNELL

"*D*id you get ahold of her?" Logan asked, coming to sit next to me on the wide leather couch that held down the far wall of the first class lounge in Chicago O'Hare.

"No," I answered, looking at my cell phone like it would hold the answers.

"Weird. Did you try texting?"

"Yeah." I thumbed through at least twelve unanswered texts. The last one she'd replied to was from this morning, and nothing had been wrong.

Was this one of those girl moments where they said everything was fine, but really they were secretly plotting your death?

"Did you do something to piss her off?" Logan raised his eyebrows.

I scoured my memory, trying to think of something— anything that would explain what the hell was going on back in Charleston. "I can't think of a single thing, honestly. Maybe her cell phone died?"

He looked away and nodded slowly. "Right. Her cell phone died and that's why she hasn't answered a call or a text in the last seven hours. Maybe she's busy. Maybe a bird got out at the reserve."

"Yeah. I'm sure it's nothing. I just wanted to tell her we'd been delayed." We'd been delayed again and again and *again*.

"We can't really control the weather," Logan said with a shrug.

"You get through to Blaire?"

"Yeah. She said something about Echo going off on her, but I'm not getting in the middle of it. I mean, Echo is pregnant and hormonal and Blaire can be… a little overdramatic." He rubbed the back of his neck and looked across the room to where Sawyer sat with Axel and Lukas.

Cannon plopped down in the overstuffed armchair opposite our couch and pulled out a book.

"But everything is good there?" I asked.

Cannon looked up quizzically.

"I was asking Logan about Blaire," I explained.

He grunted and went back to his book.

"Yeah, I mean, I think so. Don't get me wrong, she drives me batshit crazy with some things, but when it comes down to it, she puts up with our schedules and my shit, which we all know can't be easy."

"She wasn't complaining when she dropped thirty-five thousand of your money on a handbag," Cannon said without even looking up from the pages.

"Okay, that was…" Logan sighed. "That was utterly fucking ridiculous, but when push comes to shove, I guess it was important to her and it was within my means to give it to her, so why not?"

"Because you didn't give it to her, she gave it to herself?" Cannon suggested.

Logan's head tilted.

I flattened my lips and looked anywhere but at him.

"Connell gave Annabelle a hundred grand in fucking

ostriches and you have a problem with thirty-five?" Logan leaned forward, resting his elbows on his knees.

"Holy shit. Listen to what I'm saying." Cannon put his book down with obvious annoyance. "Connell gave his woman a hundred grand worth of birds. While insane and maybe a little psycho, that was a choice *he* made. Your woman bought herself a thirty-five-thousand dollar purse on your credit card. There's a difference."

"She loves me," Logan said quietly. "And that money was nothing. A drop in the bucket. So what does it matter if it makes her happy?"

"She loves your social media following," Cannon muttered.

"Don't fucking go there," Logan snapped, then turned to me. "Do you feel the same?"

Oh, bloody hell. "Why are you dragging me into this?"

"Because I want your opinion!"

"Look, if anyone said something even remotely off-color about Annabelle, I'd rip their heart out and shoot it at the net. I'm not going to say shit about your girlfriend, that's for sure." I leaned back and prayed for a miracle. For the weather to clear so we could take off, or for lightning to strike me dead. Immediately. Right fucking now. Anything to get out of this conversation.

"Okay, I'm giving you a free pass." Logan pinned me with narrowed eyes.

"There's no such thing as a free pass. No matter if you say it's a free pass or not, you'll remember exactly what I said. And then you'll marry her and it will be really fucking awkward at your wedding when you remember that I said something, and even when I tell you that you said I had a free pass, it won't bloody matter!"

"He's right," Cannon said, tapping his fingers along his

jaw. "However, I have no such problem telling you what I think."

"Already noted," Logan retorted.

"Let's try this a little differently," I suggested. "Is there anything about the lass that worries you?"

Logan's brow furrowed. "Okay, I think she's great, and she makes me really happy, but…"

"But what?" I asked.

"But I'm not thrilled with how public she makes every-thing," he answered with a shrug. "I get that she's an influ-encer—whatever the hell that means—but does the world really care what she has for breakfast? Or what I had for lunch? Does she have to post moments I think are private?"

"Nope," Cannon answered, which earned him my glare.

"But then again, that's her job, right? She's paid to post stuff. She literally makes her living posting shit on social media. She would never show up at the rink and tell me how to do my job so how can I tell her how to do hers?"

"Well, your job doesn't really involve exploiting her," I said slowly, hoping it wasn't about to lose me my friend.

He blinked, then moved like he was going to speak, only to stop and blink again. "You think that's what she's doing?"

"Exploiting you?" I clarified.

"Yes," Cannon answered. "She boosts her following by using your fame. You refuse to model, which is what-the-fuck ever, but people like to look at your face for some reason, and she has the monopoly on *you*. People follow her to see *you*. Of course she makes you happy, she can't afford not to."

Logan sat back and let his head fall against the couch. "Yeah, I know."

"You know?" I asked.

"I'm not an idiot. I know she's…used me to get ahead, but I have to ask myself how much I care, I guess."

Cannon narrowed his eyes. "I'm sorry. Say that again."

"If she makes me happy, then I should be the one to determine if the cost is too steep, right?"

"I can't argue with that." I shook my head.

"Right. She's never hurt any of you, and she hasn't hurt me, either. Do I have concerns? Sure. But I'm not blind to them." He looked at us in turn, making sure we understood his point.

"Got it," I said. "Subject is closed."

Cannon sighed and went back to his book.

"Gentlemen." Coach rubbed the skin between his eyebrows as he approached. "Grab your bags. We're staying the night. We'll get out first thing in the morning, but FAA says we can't fly in this."

We all collectively groaned.

So much for getting home—for getting to Annabelle tonight.

* * *

"Hey, lass. I'm starting to really worry that something has happened to ye. I've called a few times, and texted, but you're not responding. I thought maybe your phone was dead last night, but now it's today and you're still not picking up. God, I'm just hoping everything is okay."

"Sir, you need to hang up for take off," the flight attendant lectured with a frozen smile.

"Okay, we're finally getting ready to takeoff, so I'll come straight to you when I get home. Just text and let me know where you'll be. Please?"

"Sir."

"I love ye and I'll see ye shortly."

"Sir!"

"I'm off!" I snapped, and swiped my phone into airplane mode.

Fuck. What the hell was going on? Was she hurt? Wouldn't someone have called me? Why wasn't she answering? Had I made her angry by insinuating that I wanted to crawl into bed with her when I got home? Had she changed her mind about me? About us? Were the away games too much for her to handle?

My thoughts raged the entire flight home, and by the time we landed in Charleston, I was a balled up mess of raging nerves and fear.

"It's just the phone," I assured myself as I drove toward Sweet Water in the caravan of hundred-thousand dollar cars that made up the Reapers. "It went dead. She threw it. Arnie stole it."

She wasn't hurt. She wouldn't be. Even Sawyer said that Echo had been too busy at the bar to talk much, but if something had been wrong with Annabelle, Echo would have said something.

I pulled into my drive and felt about fifty years of stress fall off me as I spotted her white Volvo in the drive. She was here. Thank God.

I parked in the garage and didn't even bother to close the door before I flew into the house.

"Annabelle!" I called out, throwing my keys on the counter.

There was a rustling—she was coming down the stairs.

I walked into the foyer with a smile on my face. "God, I've missed ye, lass. What happened to your phone? I've been calling and calling—what the hell?"

Annabelle came down the stairs wearing jeans and a T-shirt, which was enough to alarm me, but she was carrying a box.

"Glad you made it home safely." Her voice was as cool as

the look she sent my way before walking straight past me. No smile. No kiss. Nothing.

"Annabelle? Love?" I followed her to the front door. "Where are you going?"

"Home," she answered.

"But I just got here…"

"Which is why I'm leaving. I honestly thought I'd have my stuff out by now, but it proved a bit more difficult than I thought."

"What am I missing?" I asked slowly, trying to get my brain to recognize what was causing my heart to bleed out on the hardwood.

"Missing? Well, I guess that would be me. I'm leaving."

"The house?" I guessed, hoping she didn't mean what I thought she did. The nausea churning in my belly told me it was *exactly* what I feared.

"No, Connell. I'm leaving *you*."

Forget bleeding out, my heart disintegrated on the spot.

18

ANNABELLE

"*A*nnabelle," Connell said my name like a plea as I dropped the box on his porch and spun around, heading up the stairs to get the last one. I shuffled around his bedroom, throwing the last of my things into the final box. "Annabelle, I deserve to know what the hell is going on," he said, stepping into my path to halt my progress. His touch was like a brand, and I jerked my arm from his hand.

I gaped at him, the only emotion I allowed myself to show at the moment. "You're going to pretend like you don't know?"

His eyes widened. "I have *no* idea what would cause you not to take my calls or spur this reaction." He tapped the box in my hands.

Pain rippled through my already shredded heart. Why was he still playing me? I shook my head, shifting the box to my hip to fish my cell from my pocket. A couple clicks, and the article and photos were up. I tossed it at his chest, and he caught it with fast reflexes.

The longer he scrolled, the longer her read the article, the more that muscle in his jaw ticked. The more I thought he would break my phone from clutching it so hard.

He carefully handed the phone to me, taking a step backward. "Please listen to me," he said. "You *know* I'm crazy about you. This is—"

"I said this would happen from the beginning." I scoffed, shaking my head. "I *kept* saying it. I told you all about my ex and what happened in Atlanta from long distance. Told you I would never be put in that situation again. And you...*you* had the nerve to tell I was wrong. To make me believe—" I cut my words short, pressing my lips together.

No. If I went down this line with him, all the walls I'd constructed would crumble. They'd already suffered an astounding blow at the sight of him—wild and frantic, his scent filling the air with a painful sharpness.

"Annabelle—"

"*Stop*," I cut him off. "Please stop saying my name like that."

"Like what?" he challenged, taking a step closer to me. "Like I love ye?"

Tears coated my eyes, and I nodded.

He sighed, his breath warm on my cheeks he was so close. My body vibrated from the battle of wanting to run *away* from him and *toward* him at the same time. He dared to reach a hand up and wipe a traitorous tear from my cheek.

Despite myself, I leaned into his hand.

"It's not true," he said, and reality crashed over my head.

I pulled away and walked past him, collecting the last set of pajamas from my dresser drawer across the room. I set the box atop the dresser, now filled to the brim with things that suddenly didn't seem so important. My entire relationship, summed up in the scraps of silk and lace I'd left at his house. *Scraps*—just what we were now.

I sucked in a sharp breath, mustering the courage I needed to say the words.

"Goodbye, Connell," I choked out, reaching for the box.

"Don't you dare," he said, the primal tenor in his tone reverberating inside my soul.

I spun, eyes wide. "Don't *I* dare?" I glared at him. "Connell, *do* me a favor." Good. Anger was much better than the heartbreak.

"Picture me," I continued. "Picture me with Cannon. Or Logan. Hell, picture me with those two rookies, at *once*. Their hands on me. Their lips on my skin." He flinched, but I kept going. "Now picture me *laughing* about it. Imagine reading a text where I explain how it doesn't count if you're not in the same state. Hell, not the same city."

I stepped closer to where he'd turned into a statue, the box forgotten behind me. His muscles rippled beneath his skin as he folded his arms over his chest. Pain—real and raw—flickered in his blue eyes. I ignored it, not certain what he was so upset about. Getting caught? Certainly, it wasn't over losing me or he wouldn't have done what he did.

"Feel that?" I asked, stopping a breath from his body, the tension curling from him and settling on my skin. "Now imagine how I feel thinking about you being with other women and then bragging about it?"

"I. Didn't. Do. It."

Exhaustion settled in my bones. My heart ached with the want to believe him because the pain I'd been living with for the last two days was just too much.

"You didn't do what exactly?" I asked slowly.

"I never touched those women—at least not in any way that wasn't strictly professional. I haven't put my hands on any other woman out of desire besides you since we met. I did not cheat on you."

His eyes were so sincere that I couldn't help but believe

189

him. But if he didn't cheat on me, why would he run off at the mouth that he had?

"You didn't say those things? The reporters just made it up?" I edged, hating myself for opening the door for him to crush me completely.

He visibly swallowed.

And I felt the lack of denial in my chest like a punch. I stumbled back a step, then another.

He followed me, arms outstretched between us. My back hit the dresser, and he dropped his hands at the glare in my eyes. "I did say those things," he admitted, and somehow a new fresh wave of pain sliced through my soul like an axe dropping.

Some, stupid, hopeless part of me wanted it *all* to be a lie. For him to be suing the reporters for slander.

"But it was a joke," he said. "I was trying to put this jackass in his place."

I tilted my head. "A joke?"

"Sarcasm," he clarified, raking his hands through his hair. "I was pissed off at his implications about me. About all NHL players. I lost my temper and made a joke—"

"A joke?" I narrowed my gaze. "Lost your temper?" I repeated. "By saying you loved to cheat while you were draped with a handful of half-naked, *perfect* women?" I hugged myself, tearing my gaze away from him.

"First off, they were far from perfect, and second...not my most clever move," he said. "But I was only repeating what he implied. Go talk to him! He'll tell you."

I swallowed hard. "There are *ten* other tabloids that have run the same article. *Who* exactly would you like me to speak with, Connell?"

"The *scunner* who started this bullshit," he snapped.

"*Scunner?*"

He rubbed his palms over his face. "Irritating piece of

shit," he clarified.

"You didn't cheat on me," I said the words aloud.

"Never," he said on a loosed breath. "I would *never*."

I cleared my throat, hugging myself tighter. "You just think so little of our relationship that you thought it would be *funny* to say those things. Things you knew would hurt me, *cut* me to the quick."

"Annabelle—"

"No," I cut him off. "This is almost *worse*." I swiped at the tears in my eyes. "Because you may not have cheated on me, but you clearly think so little of me, so little of our relationship, that you saw fit to use it as a *joke*. You didn't respect me enough to keep your mouth shut, for once." The words poured from me, sharp and stinging on their way out.

Connell flinched again, then glared at me. "That's not how it went down."

"Oh, really? You didn't turn our entire relationship into tabloid fodder when you could have simply said that you would never cheat on the woman you love?"

"I did! I told him that I am in a committed relationship, and then I told him that ye *trust* me, which obviously ye don't!" He backed away as he shook his head at me.

"Trust? I trusted the words you said yourself!"

"Bloody hell, woman! That was one line...okay, a few lines out of the interview! The rest of it I talked about how much I loved ye. That I don't know a single Reaper who would cheat on his woman."

"Then why would he only print this?"

"Because he's a reporter!"

"That *you* gave the quote to! You've been around enough reporters to know they'll take whatever they want from an interview, and you *gave* it to him."

"I was pissed! I'm sorry, I didn't think. I was pissed."

"Really?" I scrolled through the interview and then turned

my camera to face him. "Because you look really pissed here with all those mostly naked women spraying you down with champagne. So pissed."

His jaw ticked. "That was after he left."

"Uh. huh."

"I was happy that I'd given the arse a piece of my mind! It's a national men's magazine, and I thought the only sound-bite that would come out of that interview would be that we're not the unfaithful jerks they assume we are."

"God, she was right," I muttered, tucking the phone into my back pocket.

"Who?"

"Ginger Levenson."

"What the hell does Ginger have to do with this?" He motioned between us.

"She's your ex, right?"

"Sure, from about five years ago."

"She told me that she was never enough for you. That you always had to have more attention and exposure for your career. And she was right! God, I should have listened to her, and there I was, so smug that—"

"Enough." He ran his hands over his hair. "Ginger and I dated for a few months, and we broke up because I didn't love her, and she wanted me to. She wanted pieces of me that I wasn't ready to give away. Pieces that I've only given to ye. She doesn't know anything about the man I am now. Or am I to take the word of your ex about your current choices? That's not fair."

"Well, apparently she still knows you pretty well, because you did exactly what she warned me about! You wanted exposure? You got it. Now you're on the cover of every tabloid website." My stomach hit the floor. "A national men's magazine?"

"Aye. Men's Quarterly. That's where the original article is

published."

I took in measured breaths as my face heated. "You're telling me that when the October issue hits stands *across the country*, this article saying that you love to cheat on me will be on every grocery stand in Sweet Water? In Charleston? Around the *country?*" Oh no, no, no. Internet articles were a flash in the pan, but print was *forever*.

"Well, yes. I guess, so." He rubbed the back of his neck. "I only meant to make the point that assuming I was some playboy wasn't fair. He took my words completely out of context!"

"You made your point at *my* expense!" I jabbed my finger toward him. "My mother will see that magazine! My father! My friends! Everyone I work with and for. Everyone in my life who knows I fell in love with you will know that you *didn't*! God, it was awful knowing that they could stumble onto it online, but...I'll never live this down!"

"Annabelle, I love ye. That was never my—"

"You don't love me! You just publicly humiliated me for what? A soundbite? So you could feel better about yourself because someone dared to make an assumption? You turned what we have into a quick sarcastic comment because you couldn't resist? That's not love! Love would have been giving him a serious answer instead of having to make everything a damned joke!"

"I never thought—"

"You didn't think about me! About us! God, my mother will hear about it at the salon. The grocery store. *Everywhere*. My sister already knows, since she called a few hours ago, and it's only a matter of time before Dad has to endure pitying glances at the hardware store that his silly daughter was stupid enough to fall for the NHL star who found her convenient."

"God, Annabelle, I made a mistake, but why do you care

so much about what other people think?"

"I care what *you* think, and you told the whole world in that interview! I'm done. Because clearly, there is no other way it could've gone. And you had to have known it would end like this, right here. With me in shattered pieces, heart fully, properly broken over a man who apparently was never truly mine." My soul shuttered at my own words.

"You know me," he said. "Whether you believe it or not. You're not giving me a chance. You're making me out to be him and I'm not! You're not even going to *try* to find the truth."

"Why should I?" I snapped. "You already admitted to saying those things! And the fact that they could leave your mouth speaks volumes about how you actually feel about me."

"You know how I feel about you, Annabelle. I love you. I never loved anyone like I—"

"You don't," I cut him off before he could turn me to ash. I grabbed the box off the dresser, looking at him over my shoulder. "Because if you did? We wouldn't be *here*." Tears rolled down my cheeks at the distance between us. "I wouldn't be broken and bleeding with no cure in sight, and more coming the minute that goes to print." I choked back a sob, putting one foot in front of the other.

"Don't do this. You're supposed to be stronger than this. You're supposed to weather the storms with me, not run at the first rain drop."

"You don't get to guilt me like that. Not when you're the one who made the storm and then shoved me outside in it. Goodbye, Connell."

"Annabelle, don't do this. Give me a chance—"

"Goodbye," I said again, the word clanging through me in an ice-cold finality as I carried my broken heart down his stairs, and out his door for good.

19

CONNELL

he doorbell rang, and I raked my hand over a week's worth of beard growth as I walked to my foyer. A week. We'd played another away series and made our way home last night. A week without Annabelle's laugh or her voice. A week without her kiss or even her scorn.

It had been the longest, saddest week of my damned life.

I swung the door open and sighed as Echo filled the doorway. Her hair was growing out at the roots since she was scared to dye it while pregnant, but that was the only change I could mark in Sawyer's fiancée—besides the baby belly, of course.

"If you're here to throw things at me, ye can just walk right back across the street because I don't have the energy to duck anymore."

She looked over her sunglasses at me and sighed. "You look like shit."

"It's a reflection of how I feel," I quipped sarcastically, and then shook my head because that's what got me into this whole mess.

"Good," she said as she swung a bag from her shoulder.

"Woman, I just can't with you today."

"And what were your plans, exactly?" She tilted her head.

"Get so roaring drunk that I wake up tomorrow just so one more day goes by," I answered honestly.

"So, you're miserable?"

I bit back another sarcastic comment and sighed instead. "Aye. I'm fucking heartbroken because I said something careless that was twisted in a way that hurt the woman I love, and now she won't so much as speak to me. Is that what ye wanted to hear?"

"Yep. Now move. I'm coming in." She nodded toward the door.

I backed away out of sheer confusion. "Echo, if I wanted to see you, I would have gone to the bar."

"I know," she called over her shoulder as she walked by. Then she took out a bottle of scotch and held it high. "That's why I brought the bar to you."

After closing the door, I followed her into my kitchen, where she already had a shot poured into one of my juice glasses.

"What are you doing?" I asked as she rummaged through my refrigerator.

"Looking for—awh, these are the little teas that Annabelle likes," she held one of the teas above her head for a second and then stuck it back in the fridge.

"Aye, I kept a lot of things that she liked. Still doesn't explain why you're here."

"Here we go." She pulled out a bottle of flavored water and shut the door. "I was looking for something non-alcoholic or caffeinated so I could drink with you. Now sit." She motioned to the barstool at the end of the island.

I did.

She took out a small figurine of a grim reaper and put it

on the island, then pushed the shot into my hand. "The second location of *Scythe* is now open for business."

I arched an eyebrow at her, and she simply let her gaze flicker between mine and the shot until I took it.

The scotch burned down my throat but warmed my otherwise numb torso. Everything was numb. It was like my body had shut off all feeling out of a sense of protection.

"How is she?" I dared to ask.

Echo's eyes narrowed for a moment, but she took a drink of water and then nodded. "Heartbroken. Mad as hell. Looks a lot like you right now, actually. Sweatpants and all. Just without the beard. Figured I'd come over and see what the chances were of fixing this because I've never seen Annabelle as happy as she was when she was with you. Then again, I've never seen her as low as she is now, either."

"She doesn't trust me."

"You didn't exactly give her a reason to."

The click of the door sounded a second before someone said, "Connell?"

"I'm in here, Langley," I answered. "She's the only person who would just walk in," I said to Echo in explanation.

"Oh, good. Wait, what are you doing?" Langley came to a halt when she saw Echo pouring me another drink.

"Getting him drunk so I can wheedle the truth out of him. What are you doing?"

Langley sighed and snatched both the bottle and the glass from Echo. "Trying to dig up the truth so we can save his relationship and his reputation, which means keeping him sober."

Echo tilted her head at Langley.

Langley didn't flinch. "I love you, Echo. You know, I do. But I've known Connell long enough to know that he's not lying when he says his comment was taken out of context. And I have to have *his* best interest at heart, the same way I'm sure you have Annabelle's. So you can join team *figure-this-shit-out-for-the-good-of-all,* or you can take your cute, pregnant butt home because this is work time."

"Was it taken out of context?" Echo questioned me.

"What did she tell you?" I fired back.

"That you made a sarcastic comment that caused her abject, public humiliation on a nationwide scale."

"Aye, that part is true. But the rest of that interview talks about how much I love her. He took that one line and twisted it. And maybe I never should have said it, but I was pissed that he implied the woman I loved wouldn't be enough. That surely I had to indulge a little on the side. He implied that we *all* did, Echo, including your fiancée."

Echo stared at me so long that I thought she might flip me the bird and walk off. Instead, she dragged the other stool next to mine and sat with a muttered, "Fuck my life."

The doorbell rang, and Langley left to answer it.

"I love her," I said softly.

"I know you do," Echo replied.

"Okay, here's where we stand," Langley remarked as she came back with Persephone in tow. God, they both looked so put together—Langley in a black suit and Persephone in an obviously designer sheath dress. I thought my shirt had been clean yesterday, but I wasn't honestly sure. "We need the full interview. You said he had it on a tape recorder, right?'

"Aye."

"Okay. I got in touch with Men's Quarterly, and they said that John Perry is actually a freelance writer. He's not on staff. They said they'd pull the print like you demanded if what you're saying is correct, that he purposely skewed your words, but since all he was required to do was give them the actual piece, they don't have the interview."

"So what are we supposed to do with that?" I asked. "That tape is all I have to get back Annabelle. I couldn't give a rat's ass about my reputation, and I understand that's your job, but I want Annabelle. I need that tape."

"I know you do, that's why I brought in Persephone."

Sephie smiled. "Don't worry, Connell. I know Richard McCarthy—he owns the magazine. I'm going to slip into a room with Langley and make this call really quick with her if that's okay with you? I didn't want to interfere if you weren't comfortable."

"Interfere!" I blurted. "Please, God, interfere."

"Okay." She put her small hand on my shoulder. "I'll see if we can get this all fixed up for you." She looked up over my shoulder. "Echo, you look wonderful, just in case no one has told you today. Pregnancy looks amazing on you. Now, I'm going to sneak off with Langley."

The doorbell rang again.

"Jesus, what is this?" Echo muttered.

"Sephie, why don't you head into the study, and I'll be right in?" Langley offered as the two headed toward the front of the house.

"You were already working on getting the interview," Echo said quietly.

"Aye. It's the only way she'll believe me, and even then, she still might not forgive me. Sure, I was wrong, but the lass cares so much about what people think. Even if I pull us through this one, what's to say she won't run the next time someone twists something I say? I can't watch every single word that leaves my mouth, or I become someone I'm not. Is that really the only way she'll love me?"

Echo blinked a few times and opened her mouth to speak.

"You didn't tell me you were having a party," Logan chided as he walked into my kitchen with Cannon. "Hey, Echo."

"Boys," she said with a grin. "Did you come to harass our resident heartbreak?"

"Something like that," Logan answered, setting a bottle of water in front of me, then handing another to Cannon.

"Some friends," Echo scoffed. "At least I brought alcohol."

"He has practice in three hours. We brought hydration." Logan smirked.

"We figured you might already be piss drunk or hungover, so we gave ourselves some wiggle time." Cannon crossed his arms over his navy blue Reaper T-shirt and leaned back against the granite. "Now drink. Ward has three more bottles in that cute little backpack of his."

Logan lifted his pack with a smile.

As much as they annoyed me, they were good friends, that was for sure.

"Okay, she's working her magic," Langley said as she reappeared. "So what, did you two draw the short straws?"

Logan shrugged. "We were the only ones who weren't ready to shove the love-conquers-all pep talk down his throat."

"Even Axel?" Her eyes widened.

"Especially your husband," Cannon remarked. "The guy should work at Disney at the rate he's in the text thread talking about fate and shit."

A smile touched Langley's mouth.

"Richard, that's exactly what I'm saying," Persephone's sweet drawl filled the room, and Cannon tensed as she walked in with her phone to her ear. "Of course, I know you don't want to have to print a retraction. That's why I stepped in. I know you'd be absolutely mortified to find out that one of your employees was knowingly lying. I know how hard you worked to get that magazine to where it is."

She looked up at the men leaning against the end of my counter, and her grip slipped on her cell phone. It tumbled from her hand, but before it could hit my hardwood, Cannon caught it mid-air and gave it back to her.

"Thank you," she mouthed quietly as a male voice muttered words we couldn't hear on our end.

"I know. I really do. I'm telling you that Connell MacD-huibh is telling the truth. John Perry purposely twisted what he said. How do I know? Because I'm standing in the man's kitchen, Richard. He's a dear friend. Connell, of course, not Mr. Perry. We're friends. Have I ever, in the ten years we've known each other, lied to you?" She tilted her head to the side and nibbled her lower lip as the man gave his verdict.

She sighed and shot Langley a frustrated look with a shake of her head.

"Of course, I would never demand you cancel the print run. I know you have twenty-five million readers."

Holy shit. Twenty-five million people were going to read that I cheated on the woman I loved? Just the thought had me nauseated.

"I'm just saying that once you hear the tape for yourself, you'll probably *want* to. I mean, you own a very well respected magazine, Richard. It would just be a shame to see it turn into a tabloid. Goodness, I think it took Matt Sharpe —what was it—three years to build himself back up after that unfortunate article about the governor's wife, and I'd just die if that happened to you, Richard. We're such good friends, and I couldn't not warn you. You understand, don't you?"

A slow smile spread across her face.

Cannon's water bottle crinkled in his hand.

My breath stilled.

"Oh, I'm sure that would work. I've never known a free-lance writer to not want their paycheck. Oh, and could I ask a personal favor?" Her cheeks pinked as the voice continued at the other end. "Well, no. I'm not. He's just a family friend. No, Richard. I was actually going to ask if you wouldn't mind forwarding me a copy of that tape once you have it? It would mean so much to me."

I swallowed. God, my throat felt so tight.

"What's in it for you?" she laughed, but the sparkle wasn't there. "If you're willing to fly down, how about if we play a round at the club next weekend? Mmm hmm. Sounds delightful. I'll even bring Daddy. So nice talking to you, Richard. Give your mama my love. Bye now."

She hung up and smiled so big that the lump in my throat started to dissipate. That had to mean she got him to agree, right?

"Okay, he—"

The doorbell rang.

"Bloody hell!" I roared toward the door.

"I'll get that one." Echo pushed away from the counter and headed toward the front door.

"He said he'd hold John Perry's check until he appeared with the tape. And I know Richard, he'll cancel the print, or at least hold it up to replace the article before he opens himself up to a lawsuit."

"You didn't threaten a lawsuit," Logan noted.

"No, but I did mention our friend Matt who was sued for *millions* when he printed a fake story. He got the point, trust me." She nodded.

"You're frightening," Logan muttered.

"You're bloody *brilliant!*" I exclaimed. "God, I'd hug ye if I didn't reek."

"I appreciate the offer." She grinned, but it faded as she met Cannon's gaze. "You don't approve?"

"You want me to approve the fact that you just prostituted yourself to get a tape?" He slammed his water down on the counter.

"Cannon—" I warned, but the lass didn't flinch.

She marched right up to him in her heels and glared. "I agreed to play golf with him, Cannon. That's all."

"Sounded like he wanted a lot more than that."

"Well, he probably does, but he's not going to get it. He's been sniffing around since junior high. That's why I'm bringing my dad. He won't put up with that nonsense. He never has. Put those big muscles of yours away and use that big brain instead. He has something I want. I have something he thinks he wants. It all works out in Connell's favor. And if I'm willing to spend an afternoon in that wretch's tedious company, what business is it of yours?" She had to brush a handful of really long blonde hair back over her shoulder, ruining a little of her tirade.

He folded his arms across his chest, and I didn't miss the way her eyes followed the movement.

Oh, fuck. This wasn't good.

"It's not," Cannon confirmed.

"Goo—"

"I know he's here!" A shriek erupted from the hallway.

"Fuck me," Logan muttered and started walking that way.

"Drinks and a show," Langley mumbled as she headed for the fridge.

"What the hell are you doing here, Blaire?" Logan snapped.

"I need to talk to you!" she shouted loud enough to make me flinch. "I tracked your phone—"

"You what? Look, I said everything I needed to. We're done. Over. Finished. You told my friend's girl to make up some shit about him and post it for revenge?"

She suggested what exactly? My eyes went huge, but that shot was still warming my belly, dulling my judgment, so I sat my happy ass there.

"I told her to take her power! You guys have everything, and you just expect us to bow and scrape for you and be happy for whatever scraps you leave!" She jabbed him in the chest.

"What the hell are you talking about? I didn't expect anything from you! I gave you everything I had—"

"Not your heart! If I had that, you never would have broken up with me just because I gave a girl advice."

"You don't want my heart. You want my name and my face, and my social media following. I just wanted you...and now I'm not sure why."

Damn. Harsh.

"Oh, grow up, Logan. Everyone uses *everyone*. You wanted a doting girlfriend, so I gave that to you. I needed a platform boost, and you gave it to me." She pointed at Langley. "She used her marriage to boost her career."

"Excuse me?" Langley retorted.

"She got knocked up and now gets NHL rate child support and a fucking ring." She motioned toward Echo.

"Oh, honey, if you only knew." Echo shook her head and slid back onto the barstool next to mine.

"It's getting very daytime talk show in here," I muttered.

"You were the one who told him!" Blaire shouted at Echo.

"Yep. Zero guilt over that one. A man should know when he's in bed with a snake." She shrugged.

Blaire's jaw dropped, and her head swung, no doubt looking for another victim. "And you," she seethed at Persephone. "Perfect, Persephone-fucking-VanDoren. What the hell would you know about wanting a goddamned thing when everything you've ever wanted has been—"

"No." Cannon moved in front of Sephie, blocking her completely from Blaire. She looked up at him and quickly back-stepped.

"You need to leave, Blaire." Logan pointed toward the door. "Harass me again—harass my friends again, and I'll get a restraining order. Take your Birkus bag and your hundred-thousand followers and get out."

"Birkin bag," she corrected him with a crazed look in her

eyes. "I belong here, Logan. We can be good for each other! I can get you endorsements and—"

"Get. Out." His words were soft, but final.

"You'll see what a big mistake this all is," she tried again, her voice gentling.

"Get. Out," he repeated.

She took one last look at us—even Sephie where she peered around Cannon's chest, she was that small—and nodded. Then she turned and walked out.

We all sighed as the door clicked shut.

"Fuck, I hate women," Logan snapped.

"Hey!" Langley, Echo, and Sephie all protested like they'd been scripted.

"Not all women." His shoulders sagged. "Just the ones like that. Swear to God the next woman I date won't even know I'm damned Reaper."

Cannon moved, taking his original position at the counter.

"Thank you," she told him.

"It's not a crime to have what you've always wanted," he answered with a shrug. "Just a waste if you don't appreciate it."

"I never said I have everything I've ever wanted. She presumed. Don't make the same mistake." She cleared her throat and faced me. "Okay, back to the original problem. Richard just texted. He's getting the tape tonight. Hopefully we can stop the bogus story from printing which solves Langley's problem, but if you give the tape to Annabelle, maybe it will solve your problem, too."

"I don't know how to say thank you, Sephie."

She smiled at me. "You just did."

"Well as fun as this has been, Sephie and I are needed at our respective offices. Cannon, Logan, please see that he's sober, showered, and at practice?"

"Yes, Mom," Logan sang, but his eyes were dull.

"Echo, Connell, it was so lovely to see you, even if it was a little...dramatic. Logan, please let me know if there's anything I can do for you." She turned to Cannon. "Cannon."

"Persephone."

"Leaving," Langley announced. In a whirl of blonde hair, Sephie followed Langley out.

"That girl is like a fucking unicorn had sex with a rainbow and then that offspring mated with woodland fairy Barbie," Echo muttered.

We all turned slowly to look at her.

"What? Sawyer calls her Fairytale Princess Barbie if that helps." She shrugged.

"It doesn't." Cannon announced, then started chugging his water.

"How do Barbies mate?" Logan questioned.

"You see, when two people love each other—" I started.

He grinned. "Now look at who's back to cracking jokes."

My smile fell.

"Connell, walk me out," Echo ordered, taking her bag from the counter.

She was quiet until we reached the front door. "I was thinking about what you said."

"With all that in there, ye had time to think?"

She rolled her eyes. "Look. I don't think she wants you to change. I think she wants you to put her first. That's before your need to crack a joke or mouth off during an interview. She loves you. I know that. She wants you, Connell. Not some watered-down serious version of you. Honestly, she needs you to help her with that whole caring-what-people-think thing."

"She doesn't want anything to do with me." I scratched at my beard. "Ye think she'd even listen to the tape if I got it? That I'd even have a shot?"

"I think if you can get her to listen to the tape, and if it really talks about how much you love her, then she'd be a fool not to give you another shot. And...God, I'm going to regret this if it doesn't go right, but I'll help you in whatever way I can."

An idea sparked in my head, but it was a gamble.

A big one.

"Do ye think ye can get her to a game for me?"

ANNABELLE

*D*raped in my favorite cream cashmere sweater and thick brown editor pants, I tried to step into Reaper arena with a mask of confidence and bravado. But even with the power-outfit and heeled boots, it wasn't enough.

The past two weeks had been miserable. Every attempt from Connell to connect re-opened the wound that I doubted would ever heal. Even after many nights' sleep, drinks with Echo, and diving head-first into my work, I *missed* him. Hated that I missed him so much, hated that I spent hours staring at my bedroom ceiling coming up with ways to rationalize his behavior. Forgive him.

But what would that make me? How could I trust what we'd had was real for him? Or would everything always be some hilarious joke?

I smoothed my sweater, my heart racing. After Echo had informed me about a check Persephone had collected on behalf of the reserve, I'd almost sent Lacy to retrieve it, but while I may have a broken heart, I wasn't without my dignity.

The game had yet to start, but the stadium seats were full.

The jumbotron played clips from previous games or advertisements for concessions before the game started. Rock music blared overhead, the guitar riffs and bold lyrics pumping up the already excited crowd.

I tried not to grind my teeth as I headed to where Echo had indicated I collect the check. Down the west corridor, toward where the hallway met the ice.

Somewhere in the locker room, Connell was likely lacing up his skates getting ready to tackle the ice in the way he did best.

I cringed at the hunger to see him, to set eyes on his strong jaw, his mischievous smile, to feel those strong arms cradle me like I was the most important person in the world.

I shoved those thoughts away, reminding myself of the very real pain from his words, from the articles.

"Love," Connell's voice sounded over the speakers, the music dying, the crowd instantly hushing. "It can look and sound like a lot of things," he continued, and I whirled around, hearing him both over the loudspeakers and behind me.

And there he was in all his Reaper glory, his skates making him ten times taller than he already was. He glided toward me, smoothing over the ice like liquid silk, a microphone in his hand. He skidded to a stop, resting one hand on the partition that bordered the ice. I walked closer, my eyes wide as I tilted my head.

"This is what it sounds like to me," he said, and he shifted on his skates, pointing to his ear.

My hands flew over my mouth as his voice filled the speakers...saying words I'd *read* before. The same horrible, awful quote that had shattered my heart in the first place. Yet, reading it and listening to it were two entirely different things.

Sarcasm and anger colored Connell's tone.

And then…

"…ye can fuck right off."

Tears filled my eyes as I continued to listen, my lips parting as I stared at Connell.

"…I happen to be madly in love with the woman I have waiting for me at home."

I gasped into my hands.

"And now," Connell said as the taped recording silenced. "This is what love *looks* like for me." He pointed to the jumbotron, and I tore my gaze from him to look up.

A new video replaced the earlier advertisements and game footage. This one was recorded by Echo at the 5K when we opened the reserve. Connell, rushing up to me after the race, his ostrich costume bobbing with his movements as he scooped me up in a flurry, kissing me before racing off with me in his arms, a wide smile on his face, me laughing the whole way.

I chuckled, tears rolling down my cheeks as another clip rolled.

This one was a shot of Connell, sitting unknowingly on a bench in the locker room smiling up at my picture taped just underneath his last name. *"Connell's got a girlfriend,"* Logan's voice taunted from the other side of the camera. Connell leaped off the bench, laughter in his eyes as he tackled Logan to the ground, the camera cutting off in a shaky haste.

I dropped my hands as another clip played.

Connell filled the frame as he filmed himself in the basement of city hall. "Clearly, this chaos has needed my help for years," he said, rolling his eyes. "This is my before shot—" *my* voice in the background, shouting at him from the top of the stairs to get his Scottish butt back upstairs to mop. His eyes lit up at the sound, gazing up the stairs in a look I could only describe as…adoring.

Another clip.

"And this is my after shot," he said into the camera before panning it around the basement. Organized, sparkling, the exact dream for any city clerk. He'd revolutionized the area. "This will definitely make her life easier," he said, grinning into the camera. "But I'll do my best to shake her up every now and again."

A laugh ripped from my chest as he winked at the camera and the jumbotron filled with pictures of him and me...ones I'd never seen. The pictures he or his friends had taken when I wasn't looking, but Connell *was.*

Looking at *me.*

Those blue eyes alight with nothing but love, adoration, and perhaps lust.

Happiness.

"And," Connell said into the microphone, the collective *awes* from the crowd echoing behind him. "If you've ever doubted how I spend my time during away games..." he shifted, shaking his head at the screen.

Video after video rolled, some filmed by him, some by Logan or Cannon or Sawyer.

A succession of silly pranks—buckets of water over the Vikings on the team, Lukas and Axel laughing but livid as they chased him down arena hallways. Shaving cream on the face of those players stupid enough to fall asleep in hotel lobbies. Cannon, furiously trying to open his book, which Connell had apparently glued shut.

I actually feared for him in that clip, not exactly sure how Connell was still alive.

Nathan Noble chasing Connell—who carried a massive gear bag—through a hotel lobby, Nathan in nothing but a tight pair of athletic underwear, Logan's laugh sounding from the behind the camera as Noble screamed at Connell.

Laughter erupted from the crowd as the clips rolled on, but Connell returned his focus to me.

"I don't have time for anything else in my life, Annabelle," he said. "Just this, and you."

My knees wobbled.

"As I hope you can clearly see," he said. "I love you. And I'll always love you."

Another wave of *awes* soared through the crowd.

"Will ye have me?" he asked, hand outstretched toward me over the partition, his eyes vulnerable and raw.

My heart soared, love pooling within every inch of my soul, knitting together all the shattered, jagged pieces that had plagued me since that stupid article had hit.

I could not deny the proof he'd collected.

Or the simple fact that he'd just laid our relationship bare in front of a sold-out arena...and I didn't care. No mortification. No worry of what the audience thought. I only wanted *him*. Nothing else mattered.

And I suddenly felt like the biggest ass in the world for being the last person to see it, to realize how he felt about me.

The same way I felt about him.

I choked back a sob, my feet propelling me toward him.

He dropped the mic on the ice, the crowd hissing from the quick assault on their ears, but soon they were cheering. Because Connell hauled me over the waist-high partition separating us, our lips a frantic and hungry meeting.

"I'm sorry," I said between kisses. "I'm so sorry, Connell. I'm an idiot. I can be so blind—"

"Don't," he said, kissing me again. "Never again," he said.

"Never again," I promised, crushing my lips against his, my body flooding with heat and happiness and need.

The roaring crowd brought us right back to earth, and I buried my face in his shoulder.

"After the game," he said, eyebrows raised. "Wait for me?"

I nodded as he gently set me back on solid ground. "Always," I said.

He grinned that damn smirk of his, skating backward on the ice, his fists raised in victory as the crowd chanted his name over and over again.

And I couldn't contain my smile or my laugh at the sight of my Reaper.

"Can I take ye home, now?" Connell asked as he came into the office Gage McPherson had so kindly let me wait inside —after handing me the check for the reserve that had brought me here in the first place.

Connell's hair was still damp from his shower after the resounding win the Reapers had just delivered.

"Lock the door," I said, slightly breathless.

Connell flashed me a half-smile, quickly locking the door behind him.

I hopped onto the desk, careful not to disturb anything behind me.

He cocked a brow as he stalked toward me. "Thought ye said you'd never be caught in public like this?"

I bit my bottom lip. "You're worth the risk."

His eyes shuttered at my words, his hands gentle as they snaked around my back as he stepped between my opened legs.

"You're worth *everything*, Connell," I said with more sincerity. "And I'm *so* sorry. I shouldn't have believed the article. I shouldn't have *cared* what anyone else thought. You mean more to me than the prospect of anyone's judgment." I shook my head. "I won't ever let anyone do that to us again. Open communication from here on out. I trust you. And I'm sorry for this broken piece of me that put us through this hell. I promise I'll work on it. If you'll have me." I sighed. "Never again?" I repeated our earlier promise.

"Never again." He pressed his forehead against mine. "I missed you."

"I love you," I breathed the words against his mouth, and he came *unhinged*. Unleashing himself on me in a flurry of lips and tongue and teeth. I gasped as he made quick work of dropping both our pants, shoving my lace to the side and sliding into me in one, smooth motion. His hands palmed my ass, leveraging my body on the desk as he pumped into me.

Each thrust a promise.

Each gasp from me an apology.

I wrapped my arms around his neck, pressing myself as close to him as humanly possible. I claimed his mouth in the same way he claimed my body, working me up in a frenzy of thrusts and caresses. Drunk on the taste of him, I spiraled toward that sweet edge, begging him for more, more, *more.*

He obliged, his eyes on mine as drove into me like a man on a mission to brand himself on my soul. And damn me if he didn't do just that. I clawed at his back, lightly biting his lip as pleasure coiled inside me.

Connell felt the shift, felt me plunging toward that explosive moment, and covered my mouth with his own, swallowing my would-be moans like his favorite drink.

I clenched around him, coming hard and fast as he took me deeper until his release quickly followed.

Our chests heaved as he held me, planting kisses along the column of my neck, the line of my jaw, and finally my lips.

I tangled my fingers in his hair, our eyes locking.

"Forgive me?" I asked, needing to hear him say the words. Needing him to absolve me of this flaw—of being blind and not giving him a chance to explain until I'd hurt us both.

He shook his head, and my heart lurched.

"Nothing to forgive, love," he said, brushing his lips over mine. "My life...the public parts of it. I can't promise they won't come after us again. But I can promise you one thing."

I swallowed hard, clinging to him with a held breath.

"I'll love you forever."

I smiled against his mouth. "Today," I said, planting a kiss on his lips. "Tomorrow." Another quick kiss. "And forever," I promised him, and sealed the vow with a slow, deep kiss that made both of us forget how to speak at all.

EPILOGUE

Connell

Six Months Later

*L*ate June was just as hot in South Carolina as I'd remembered it from last year.

"Thanks for coming to get me. Annabelle couldn't get away from the office," I told Logan as we pulled into my driveway.

"It's no problem. Really. I've missed your ugly mug for the last few weeks. It was a good trip home?" His eyes flickered toward the house.

My hackles rose just like they did every time a Reaper tried to pull a prank on me. They had yet to pull it off because I was just that damn good at sniffing them out.

"Aye. It was nice to see my mum and introduce her to Annabelle. She left about a week ago to come home for work." I put my hand on the door handle. "Everything okay?"

"Oh, yeah," he assured me with a shrug.

My mind raced. Who else could be in on it? Only Annabelle had a key to my house, so that was safe. Had they broken into the garage? Covered my car with saran wrap? Fake a fake trade contract like I'd done to Sterling earlier this year?

"Okay, well, I'm going to go inside now," I said calmly before opening the door.

"Have a good night. Let me know if you need anything." His gaze flew to the left.

Cannon's house?

Cannon was the least likely of all of them to prank me.

Logan popped the trunk, and I grabbed my bag before shutting his hatch.

"See you!" he said with a giant grin. Then he pulled out of my driveway and headed toward his house, leaving me standing in my driveway with my bag and too many questions.

I popped out my cell and dialed, then punched in the garage code.

"Hey love, just wanted to tell ye that I'm home," I said as the door rose.

"Yay! I'm at work, but I'll see if I can duck out early. I've missed you."

Her voice slid over my heart like velvet. "I've missed ye, too. You know, Logan was acting weird. I'm thinking he's trying to pull a prank on me." I examined my car, but there was...nothing. Everything looked just like it had when we left for Scotland weeks ago.

"Really?"

"He's always wanted to get me back from the time I replaced the deodorant in his stick with cream cheese."

"You did what?" She laughed.

"It was good. Trust me." I opened the kitchen door and

sighed in relief. "It must have been a false alarm." I set my keys down on the counter and walked into the living room. All clear. Then I headed toward the entry.

"Oh, good. Look, I need to go over these new contract—"

"Holy fucking shite!" I exclaimed as I walked into the formal living room. Every piece of furniture was bolted to the ceiling. "The entire bloody room is upside down!"

"What?" she exclaimed.

"Those *dobbers* put our living room on the ceiling!" I turned under the furniture, both horrified and oddly impressed.

"*Dobbers?*"

"Never you mind," I blurted. That wasn't exactly something you told a lady.

"Okay, I'm just going to come home now."

"When is the last time you were here?" I asked as I walked up the stairs, petrified of what else I might find.

"A couple of days ago? I'm so sorry, love, but you know my house is closer to work."

"Don't worry. Just get here when you can."

We hung up, and I cringed as I opened the master bedroom. "You have to be fucking kidding me," I muttered as ball pit balls raced into the hallway from where they had to be two feet deep in my bedroom. "I swear, if that keeps me from Annabelle, I'm going to kill you all."

The first guest room had bubble wrap around every piece of furniture, and packing peanuts all over the floor. "You guys are so dead," I promised quietly.

The next guest room had lollies taped to every square inch of the wall. *Taped.*

By the time I reached the final guest room, my blood pressure was up at least ten points. There was a slight humming sound, and I cringed as I opened the door.

There was a bloody bouncy castle from wall to wall. No

furniture. Nothing. Just a netted castle with a giant clown on the top.

"Connell?" Annabelle's voice came from down the hall.

"I'm at the end of the hall," I answered, still staring at the castle, wondering where the hell the motor was to shut this thing off.

"Oh. My. God." Annabelle laughed.

I turned around and my shock faded as I saw her. Those glorious curls were up off her neck, and her dress reminded me of a fifties pin-up. "God, I've missed you."

Gathering her in my arms, I kissed her senseless. She tasted like apricots and Annabelle. Our mouths moved in a ravenous harmony, each pushing and retreating in time until we both panted for breath.

"Wait," she breathed, stepping out of my arms. "Aren't you mad? I mean, there's a bounce house in the guest room!" She looked at the monstrosity with narrowed eyes.

"Aye, a little, but mostly I'm just impressed. The lads have never been able to prank me."

"Never?" She smirked.

"Not once." I shook my head. "My record at the rink was untarnished until now."

Her smile widened, and then she started laughing.

Those prank-seeking hackles raised. "Annabelle Clarke."

"At least your record remains perfect...at the rink!" She busted out laughing, and I stood there staring at her open-mouthed.

"Ye did this?"

She nodded, still laughing.

"Och. From that time I gave ye the tour."

Again, she nodded, but this time she looped her arms around my neck. "Want to take a tour with me?"

"Aye. I think you'd better show me what you've been up to, my sweet little innocent Annabelle."

She pressed a kiss to my lips, then took my hand. "This is because you are never what I expect."

"Aye, that was a wee bit unexpected," I admitted.

She led me down the hall, and I followed, watching the sway of her hips. It might have only been a week, but I was desperate for her.

"This room—" she pointed into the room full of lollipops. "Is because from that first day, I was a sucker for you."

I chuckled softly but melted a little. That had to have taken her hours.

Her smile was radiant as she looked back at me and then led me to the next guest room. "So you have to remember to handle me with care."

The bubble wrap.

"And promise to stay just as playful as you are now," she pointed to the ball pit that was our bedroom. "Because sometimes, I take life too seriously."

My hand still holding hers, she led me down the steps to the living room. "You turned my life upside down, Connell MacDhuibh," she told me with a soft kiss.

When the kiss shifted, becoming deep and thoroughly arousing, she pulled back and led me to the hallway.

"And all I see now is...well, you." She pointed.

I laughed out loud. Somehow I'd missed that she'd replaced every single photo down my wall with my headshot from my rookie year.

"You are utterly, completely brilliant." I ducked for a kiss, but she spun away, walking right through the front door.

I followed her. How the hell could I not?

"Holy hell."

Every one of our friends stood at the end of our driveway, each holding a poster board that when put together, spelled HAPPY B-DAY.

Oh. God.

She was going to be so embarrassed. It wasn't my birth-day. Not even close. This...oh shit. What was I supposed to do?

I tried to pick my jaw up off the floor and close my mouth, but I was stumped. She'd done all this work, and it was going to make her feel so—

"Is there a problem love?" she asked, winding her arms around my waist with a wide grin.

"Um...No...it's...It's perfect, Annabelle." I hugged her to me and looked over at my friends with wide eyes. Didn't at least one of them know that I was a November guy?

"You sure?" She looked up at me with mischievous eyes.

"You are completely perfect." I kissed her in full view of everyone, much to their cheering. I lifted my head, releasing her lips with remorse. "But love, I need you to know—"

"Look again," she urged.

My brow puckered, but I did as she asked. The signs had been flipped, and the two on the end were now blank. The rest spelled out MARRY ME.

I jolted, swinging my gaze back to lock with hers. "It's the 25th of June," she said softly. "A year ago, you started a six-week community service term with me, and I fell hopelessly in love with you. Now I'm wondering if you might want to sign up for a life sentence." Her smile shook.

She'd done all of this, and was...proposing? My heart stopped.

"Are ye proposing to me, lass?" I cupped her cheeks with my hands.

She nodded nervously, excitement shining clear and bright in her eyes.

"You know I'm supposed to be the one who does that, right?"

She nodded again but didn't shy away. She really was

doing this in front of our friends, facing her worst fears for me. "I figured that nothing about us has been traditional."

Well, she certainly had that right.

"Aye, Annabelle, I'll marry ye. But only if you let me run upstairs and get the ring I already bought ye." It was classic, just like she was, and had been waiting patiently for the right time to shine.

Leave it Annabelle to surprise me.

"That's a yes?" She bounced up on her toes.

"It's always a yes when it comes to ye. Yes to marrying ye. Yes to building a life. Yes to forever." I swept her up in my arms and kissed her deep, savoring the taste of joy on her tongue.

Then I waved to our friends and carried Annabelle into our home, where I promptly shut the door on them. Forevers were something you started in private.

And this was most definitely our forever.

GRINDER SNEAK PEEK

If you love the Reapers, you'll love Gage! Turn the page for a peek at the first chapter of Grinder and learn how the hottest player in the NHL became the Reapers' coach!

CONNECT WITH ME!

Text SAMANTHA to 77222 to be the first to know about new releases, giveaways, & more!

Sign up here for my newsletter for exclusive content and giveaways!

Follow me on Amazon here or BookBub here to stay up to date on all upcoming releases! You can also find me at my website here!

GRINDER

GAGE

Getting a three-year-old to sleep should be an Olympic event.

"Is that better?" I asked Lettie, smoothing back her thick brown hair from those summer blue eyes as she drained the small glass of water. She nodded, her smile full of tiny, gapped teeth as she settled back against her pillow.

If hockey was my world, where I made my living breathing the game, the ice, the needs of my team, then Lettie was my sun—the only thing in this universe that thawed my heart.

She was also the only thing I'd ever be caught waxing poetic about, but I couldn't help it, I was owned by a tiny three-year-old.

"Thank you, Daddy," she said, but the way she plucked at her covers and wiggled her tiny feet told me there was something else on my daughter's mind.

"What's up, sunshine?" I asked.

She looked up with excited eyes. "I like that Bailey is here."

"Me too," I said, unable to stop the smile that spread across my face at her happiness.

"I like Bailey."

A small chuckle rumbled through my chest. "Well, me too," I said, ruffling her hair.

"And now she's here all the time? Mornings and everything?"

"Yep," I answered, reaching for her bedside table. Bringing Bailey to live with us as Lettie's full-time nanny was a no-brainer. As often as I'd need her to travel with me for away games, and with the unpredictability of my schedule, it was really the only way for her to have a life...for either of us to. She'd been doing the job for six months already, but with the season starting up, it was the right time.

"So when I get up she'll be here?"

I paused before turning out the light and took a deep breath. "Yes, but Lettie, let's wait until the clock has a seven on it, okay? Not everyone likes to party at five a.m."

She bounced slightly, her eyes lighting with mischief. "I just can't wait to see her."

"You just saw her, remember? She tucked you in," I said, bringing her covers back up to her chin and urging her to lay down.

"I know, wasn't it amazing?"

I leaned forward, kissing her forehead. "Yes, it was amazing. And it will be amazing again tomorrow night."

"She's the best," she said, her eyes as wide as her smile. "Maybe she wants to see me before the sun is up!"

I pursed my lips, fighting the laughter that came so easily around my daughter, but only her. "Scarlett McPherson, you leave Bailey alone until morning. Do you understand me?"

Her lower lip extended in the cutest damn pout. "Yes, Daddy."

"Okay. I'm going to run for a little bit, so if you need me I'll be in the gym, okay?"

She nodded and flung herself forward, hugging me tight.

I held her close, savoring the smell of her strawberry shampoo, and the simple joy she emanated. Everything was simple in her world—her daddy loved her and Bailey adored her.

For the first time since she was born, there was a sense of stability in this house, and by God, I was going to keep it that way.

"I love you more than the stars," she said with a hard squeeze.

"I love you more than the moon."

"The stars are prettier," she argued.

"Well, the Earth needs the moon, so I love you more."

Her face scrunched momentarily before she shrugged. "Okay. But only because you need a win."

I hugged her again and put her to bed, silently cursing Rory for saying that yesterday when he was here, arguing to let Bailey move in.

I turned off Lettie's light and shut her door softly behind me.

My watch read 8:15 p.m. I could get in a couple miles and then meet the guys for drinks. Or I could get a couple miles in and maybe chill for the night.

Yeah, the second was probably the more responsible of the choices.

The refrigerator shut as I passed the kitchen, and I turned to see Bailey unloading a bag full of groceries. Her top was perfectly respectable, but the slight dip in her neckline gave me a mouth-watering glimpse of her cleavage.

Don't look at her like that, you asshat.

"Hey," I said, instead, as smooth as a fucking seventh-grader.

"Hey," she answered with a bright smile as I leaned across the island. "So I picked up some more of that Greek yogurt you like, and some stuff for cupcakes tomorrow. I figured I'd bake with Lettie to kind of celebrate our little..." she gestured around her, "arrangement?"

A corner of my mouth lifted in a smile. "Bailey, you're living with us. There's nothing illicit going on."

Pink stained her cheeks and damn if it didn't make her even more beautiful. Not that Bailey needed the help. She was petite but packed a powerhouse body that had found itself under mine in a few of my more drunken fantasies. And that face? Damn, she was perfection—huge hazel eyes, thick lashes, and olive skin with the most kissable mouth I'd ever laid eyes on.

But that was all I was ever going to lay on her.

"Well, yeah," she said, pulling her long, dark brown hair into some kind of knot on the top of her head. "It's just a transition."

"Hopefully a good one." It had to be. Lettie adored Bailey, and we'd been friends since we were kids, so it wasn't like I could afford to piss off Bailey...or our mothers.

"It will be," she promised. "Besides, I was practically living here anyway. Now I don't have to drive back to my place in the traffic."

"Agreed." Seattle traffic could be a nightmare.

She paused, leaning back against the opposite counter, inadvertently putting those lush curves on display.

Fuck my life. If I didn't get out of here I was going to sport wood harder than the fucking floor.

"I'm going to go get a couple miles in," I told her, pushing back from the island.

She reached over and into the fridge, then tossed a bottle of water my direction. "Have a good run. Oh, and I heard Rory and Warren talking today while we were moving in. If you want to grab a couple beers with the guys, I'm totally okay here with Lettie."

"Thanks. I'll think about it, but I'm pretty sure I'm just going to turn in." *And get the hell away from you before I lose my nanny to sexual harassment.*

"Okay, well the offer always stands. I don't mind." She crossed her arms under those perfect breasts. "It's not like I have a boyfriend or much of a social life outside Jeannine and Paige."

I opened the water bottle and took a few quick chugs. "Yeah, and your friends are always welcome here. Seriously. This is your house now, too."

Her smile was small but genuine. "That means a lot."

I nodded awkwardly. "I'll catch you later."

"Later."

I ran out of there so fast the room may as well have been on fire and headed down to the lowest level of the house until I got to my gym. The floor-to-ceiling windows opened up to a view of Lake Washington, where the sun was in that last moment of setting.

I powered on the treadmill, slipped my earbuds in, turned up the Eminem and hit it. My heartbeat was steady as my feet pounded at the machine beneath me, my breathing even. Maybe I wasn't that badly out of shape after all.

After taking most of the last season off when I tore the fuck out of my shoulder, I wasn't sure I'd ever get back to the Sharks, but the coach kept me on the roster, and I was still leading for my position if that baby of a rookie didn't beat me out for it.

Fuck that, it's mine.

Yeah, six months ago I couldn't have run at this speed without screaming in agony. Six months ago I'd still been in a sling, still broken as fuck from the way Helen left us.

And then Bailey had walked back into my life, fresh out of

her graduate degree at Cornell. It wasn't fate, I wasn't fucking stupid. It was our mothers pushing us together, not romantically—they weren't stupid either—but I needed help, and Bailey needed a job until she figured out what the hell she was going to do with her life...and her double degree in Art and Philosophy.

It had been perfect until I'd seen her again. The girl she'd been while we grew up, while I went to college at U-Dub and she went Ivy...well, she was long gone. It wasn't like she'd had one of those chick-flick makeovers, no, she'd always been pretty, doe-eyed, and just as beautiful inside than out. But now...

Fuck, now she was a knockout and seemed unaware of it somehow.

And worse, it was like my body had fucking Bailey-radar. She came into a room, I got hard—even when I reminded my body that she was a no-go.

It wasn't that I didn't like sex.

Fuck, I loved sex.

I adored women.

I fucked a lot of women.

Then they left.

The first woman I'd ever loved had left while I begged her to stay...

Now they left because I told them to...Let's be fair, it's not like they didn't know that was part of the package while I was dropping their panties.

I said I fucked women...I didn't fuck *over* women.

There was a difference.

Of course, they were all blonde lately. Anyone blonde or red-haired, but never brunettes. Never anyone I could accidentally mistake for Bailey.

I was never going *there,* and it didn't matter how badly my dick begged otherwise.

If she wasn't off limits because we'd grown up together—our mothers were best friends—she was definitely unfuckable because at the heart of everything, she belonged to Lettie.

And I didn't steal anything from my daughter.

Hell no, she deserved the world, and that was exactly what I was going to give her.

At mile number three, I ripped off my shirt, wiping the sweat off my forehead before tossing it and hitting two more miles. Nothing like a little run to get out some sexual frustration.

It would pass. I'd get used to having Bailey here. She'd become like a sister, and all these sexual urges would fade. It wasn't like she had them. Fuck, then we'd both be in trouble.

But it was just horny-as-hell me, lusting after the girl I'd never had, and I wasn't a little boy anymore. I was a full-grown man, a forward for the Seattle Sharks NHL team, and the best damned grinder in the league. More importantly, I was Lettie's dad, and since her mother had about as much maternal instinct as a fucking rock, I was all Scarlett had.

I had to be enough.

Better than enough.

I had to be everything.

Mile six sounded, and I lowered the speed of the treadmill, rolling my shoulders and stretching out my muscles before I headed up to the shower.

That was exactly what I needed. I congratulated myself for running out my baser needs instead of jumping my nanny as I walked up the stairs. Look at me, all civilized and shit.

I was so focused on my feet that I didn't realize Bailey was on the steps to the third floor until I nearly ran into her.

"Shit, I'm sorry," I said, catching her very smooth, very bare shoulders.

"Oh, my fault! Lettie asked for more water, so I took her up a glass," she said, but I barely heard her.

Fuck my life. Is that what she slept in? The light purple silk shorts barely covered her thighs and the spaghetti straps on the matching top looked flimsy enough to break. With my teeth.

One. Good. Bite.

"Gage?"

My eyes slid shut. Why did my name sound so damn good coming from her mouth?

I felt her fingers softly graze my sweat-dampened skin.

"Hey, are you okay? Is it your shoulder?"

I swallowed and opened my eyes, shaking my head with a forced smile. "Nawh, I'm okay."

Her eyes were wide, flecks of gold among the swirls of green as she examined my chest, tugging her on lower lip with her teeth. "Are you sure? I mean...I could ice it for you, or rub it down?"

Her forehead puckered at the same moment my dick hardened at the thought of her gorgeous, talented hands on me—hands that created masterpieces of abstract art. God, the last thing I needed was having those hands on my skin.

Apparently the run hadn't worked as well as I'd thought.

I needed to fuck her out of my head before I screwed up the one good thing I had going.

"You know, I think I will head out for a little bit. You okay with Lettie?" I asked, looking anywhere but the braless breasts that rose and fell in my face with her breaths.

"Yeah, of course. No rush. Try to relax, okay?"

I nodded, then nearly cursed as a thought came to me. "Shit, sometimes I bring women home..."

She laughed slightly. "I'm well aware of your nocturnal activities. This is your home, Gage. Feel free to..."—she flung her hands out— "do whatever it is you do. Seriously, no judgment."

I nodded again—like an idiot—and retreated up the stairs before I could further make an ass out of myself, or tell her why I really needed to get out.

A shower and a fresh change of clothes later, I was speeding away from my house in the Aston Martin toward my best friends and women who wanted the one thing I was capable of giving: my body.

No judgment, she'd said.

Hell if I wasn't judging myself for this one, though.

ABOUT THE AUTHOR

Samantha Whiskey is a wife, mom, lover of her dogs and romance novels. No stranger to hockey, hot alpha males, and a high dose of awkwardness, she tucks herself away to write books her PTA will never know about.

ACKNOWLEDGMENTS

Thank you to my incredible husband and my awesome kids without which I would live a super boring life!

Huge thanks must be paid to all the amazing authors who have always offered epic advice and constant support! Not to mention creating insanely hot reads to pass the time with!

Big shout out to A.H. for making this shine. And thank you to each and every single one of you AMAZING readers who love the these books as much as I do!

Made in United States
North Haven, CT
28 April 2022

18656408R00150